TAMARA LEMUS

Runaway Fae

First edition

ISBN: 979-8-9917849-0-0

This book was professionally typeset on Reedsy.
Find out more at reedsy.com

For anyone who has never felt good enough. Don't let imposter syndrome win. You are magical.

Chapter One

Orphan. It's the magic word I use to get people to stop asking me about my family. Do I feel bad for lying? Of course! However, the truth is too much for any human to understand. How do you explain to a mortal that your family tree includes an evil fae king and that king is your father? Imagine the look on their face when I make my introduction.

"Hi! My name is Princess Corvina Morticia Umbra, daughter of Castro Umbra, the evil fae king of the Shadow Court."

Imagine the confusion! I refuse to explain how fairies are real, I'm not a professor. Not only are we real but we live in a land called Aebriera that is sectioned into different courts. It's all just too much explaining to do and frankly, I don't want to be seen as a crazy lady. There are designated places here for people like that and I heard they are not fun.

So orphan it is! What is it with humans and their need to have everyone's backstory? This is why I tend to steer clear of humans. I remember the day I decided to come here, the whispering of Mami and Papi catching my attention. Their conversation sounded so serious.

I was roaming the halls of our obnoxiously large home when I overheard them talking in the throne room. Is eavesdropping wrong? Absolutely. Did I do it anyway? Of course, I did! I hid behind the wooden double doors that were cracked open, poking my head in enough for me to see them, without them seeing me. Mami was kneeling in front of Papi, her floor-length gown swallowed her whole due to her petite frame. I was always jealous of how short she was and cursed the Gods for giving me my father's height. There was devastation on her face, a feeling I'd never seen her express. She was never one to show emotions other than anger when my father didn't listen or pride when our army won a battle.

"It's not fair mi corazón." She was gripping his hand so tight that her knuckles were white.

"Yo sé mi alma. If I could I would stay with you for an eternity but that is not what the Gods have in store for me. The royal healer has made it clear. I am dying but that does not mean that you are alone. Corvina will be queen and you will help her rule just as you have with me." He caressed her face with his thumb, catching her tears.

Her cries became more violent as he spoke. Suddenly, her sobbing stopped, being replaced by her dark power. It encircled her, the sorrow gone and quickly been replaced by pure rage. She collected herself, ready to fight as always. That's one of the things I knew my Papi loved about her. I knew his heart would break when he saw her trying to fight a battle she could not win. It would be the first one she's ever lost. Mortals have one thing right in their myths and fables of my kind. We are immortal, but that does not mean we are without sicknesses.

Humans have their cancer and we have something similar. Whispering Delirium is a sickness that slowly eats at your mind until nothing is left. Healers have tried for centuries to figure out its cause and find a cure but with no success. You'll hear whispers of loved ones that deceive you into harming yourself or others, making you go mad and questioning yourself over what is real. It's a rare disease that I wouldn't wish upon my worst enemy. Our immortality is a gift and Whispering Delirium was our curse. It's a death sentence, untreatable no matter how much magic you throw at it but knowing my mother she'll throw everything she has at the disease if it means saving the love of her life.

Mi mama, Carmela, is something special and I'm not just saying that because I'm her only daughter. Papi went centuries without taking a mate until he met her. I am unsure if it was her beautiful tan skin, curvy body, or the kindness with a hint of badass that gleamed from her hazel eyes but as soon as their eyes met he staked his claim on her and her on him. It's a story that I grew up listening to, instead of reading actual books to me at bedtime Papi would retell their love story.

Humans have their Romeo and Juliet and I have my Carmela and Castro. The main difference between my parents' love story and Romeo and Juliet's is that when their families decided they disapproved of their love they slaughtered them. Every one of my parents' family members was killed by both their hands. Their story is the reason why I often felt like the black sheep. I would never murder anyone due to a difference of opinion but without them, I wouldn't exist so who am I to judge? I often wonder why they disapproved of their romance. Was it because they saw what would happen if their powers were to combine? Did they know how powerful their bond would make them? Carmela the strong fae warrior, is known for the carnage that she leaves in her wake, besides the most powerful dark fae kings the Shadow Court has ever known.

I hate that leaving Aebriera to dodge the crown meant leaving them behind, but I saw no other option. Everything in me told me to run. Papi might be the king of the Shadow Court but I always came first to him. He's the one constant in my life, the person I can always count on. He played with me when I was lonely, and listened to my boy troubles, even though his solution was always to kill them. Now I had to leave him forever, I'm leaving him when he'll need me the most and it felt like the biggest betrayal. I've always been my Papi's girl, doing everything right by him and now I'm breaking all the rules. It will be worth it, is what I kept repeating to myself. The thought of becoming queen and having Mami constantly analyzing me makes my skin crawl. Don't get me wrong, I love her, but I've always felt unworthy around her. I know that feeling will only intensify when I become queen.

The mortal realm is somewhere I knew my parents and none of their arm guards would think to look for me. I convinced them I hated the humans as much as they did. Like most faes, they also raised me to be hateful toward them. "Humans are trash! Humans are less than us and they hate us for it!" They would yell at me.

I would go into the study and look up books that we had on humans always in awe at the photos I saw. How can they resemble us yet be so different? Humans aren't welcomed into Aebriera, the reason my world even exists is because of them. Humans forced us into hiding long ago and ever since there has been bad blood between our kind. The sad part is, that only the fairies remember, humans only think of us as kids' tales. We were wiped from their history books even though we were once allies in many battles. Humans are constantly threatened by things they cannot control or understand. Though I know the history behind the disdain of mortals, I still could not hate them how my family wanted me to. I would never want to be punished for my family's actions, so why do the same? Human or not we are not what our ancestors were, I know I am nothing like my family. I never understood why my parents found joy raining down their terror. They're experts on making our people's fear a source of power. He would cross over to the human realm to bring them back and hunt them for sport as Mami watched along popcorn in hand.

The first thought that ran through my mind when I overheard about Papi being sick wasn't sadness but panic. Pure panic and fear of knowing that I'm his only kin, "his little legacy" is what he calls me. How am I supposed to rule the Shadow Court with the same iron fist that he has? I'm forcing his hand by leaving. He'll have no choice but to crown my mother as queen. She would agree to rule to honor him and do so with an iron fist just as he had for centuries. She could handle that kind of power, she could handle being queen way better than I could. After all, she was already helping my father with some tasks when asked. I am fully aware of the hypocrisy of my actions, to force the crown upon her head, but I am not queen material. I might come from royalty but I am convinced that something is seriously wrong with my DNA. No matter how many classes they give me or how many times they remind me that I was born to rule.

I'm fully aware that this is the coward's way out but maybe that is who I truly am, Corvina the coward. My people deserve better than a coward. Who would want a queen who was unsure of herself? I asked my parents if I could refuse the crown if I wished to, vouching for Mami to take my place.

"She would be a great queen, but that is not how this works. Our people will not accept her as queen." Papi said. I looked him straight in his dark brown eyes, the same ones that stare at me when I look at my reflection, ready to give him my very thought-out rebuttal.

"But Papi, how can you say that if you never entertain the idea? The people might surprise you. They love her just as you do."

He didn't bother to reply, he just dismissed me from his office. He's my Papi so I love him of course... but he can be a real stubborn man and a pain in my ass. Of course, after getting a stern no from Papi, I went to Mami.

"Hija mía. If I could I would. I know this is a heavy burden and I would love to take that burden from you." She planted a kiss on the forehead.

And with that, my fate was sealed. I was to be queen one day and there was nothing they would do to stop that from happening. So I sought help from elsewhere. I started making frequent visits to Oracles. Oracles can see all, past, present, and future, yet when I ask them about mine it's like I don't exist to them.

"My child, I do not see you." is all that was said by multiple Oracles.

That brings us to now. Corvina running away from her responsibilities

"I guess we should tell Corvina," Mami said, looking into the mirror on the wall to check her makeup.

My father gave her a soft kiss, eyes cold as he did, refusing to show emotion. He tried his best to give her a sense of calm as if to show her that he was not scared of what was to come. He grabbed her hand, kissing it before guiding her to my room. I quickly scurried away, hoping they wouldn't catch up to me.

My room, my place of sanctuary, the one area of the house that's fully mine. The walls were covered in ornately carved wood paneling and were accompanied by the bookshelves I hung up. In the corner of the room was an alcove with a huge stained glass window. It's where I spent most of my time, looking out into my world while reading about those worlds of fiction that I loved so much. In the center of the room across from the fireplace is my black four-poster bed with purple curtains hanging from the posts. The bed was covered in matching satin sheets, making waking up from a night's rest almost impossible. I sat in my bed pretending to read a book when there was a soft knock on my door before they entered hand in hand.

Mami spoke first. "Mi amor, we need to talk." She told me what I already knew. I gasped, pretending to be shocked.

Though I was acting, the tears that formed in my eyes were real. My Papi, the epitome of strength, will soon be a memory. Papi started to explain what was in store for me when death came for him. He was no longer my loving father, he was now in king mode; making sure that his other baby, his kingdom, wouldn't crumble in his absence.

"Your training will start tomorrow." He told me in the same voice he used while barking orders to his warriors.

I didn't bother to argue, nodding my head in understanding as I kissed them both on the cheek and squeezed them tightly. The hug lingered because I knew it would be the last one I would give them.

"It's going to be okay. You will be the best queen our people have ever seen." Papi whispered in my ear before I let go.

"Can I have a minute alone before dinner?"

They both silently nodded their heads. The click of the door started the clock; the race was on. I scrambled around my room in a frenzy. I grabbed the blade my Papi gifted me, tucking it away for safekeeping. It was the one thing I was sure I needed to pack for my journey to the mortal realm.

Chapter Two

Traveling to the mortal realm is easy if you possess the type of magic I do. My brand of magic can be described with one simple word, powerful. Powerful magic runs through my veins, it has since I was conceived. It's one of the many perks of being born within a powerful family. I've been training since I was in diapers on controlling my magic and successfully fighting and winning in combat. While my childhood was never boring, it was lonely. I remember begging my parents for a sibling. Mami would shake her head and tell me I was enough, while Papi told me he was trying, making me cringe disgustingly at the thought of them 'trying'. A snap of my fingers is all it took for me to open the black portal. I've snuck over plenty of times without my parents knowing. It was the one rule I consistently broke.

The first time I visited the humans was out of pure curiosity. It was two years ago yet the memory is still so crisp in my mind. I welcomed the winter air, snow covered every inch of the city and all the humans were bundled up in their heaviest coats. I was scanning my surroundings in awe, all my senses working overtime to ensure I didn't miss anything. The smell of food coming from a cart that sold something called hot dogs, the buzzing sound of traffic, and humans yelling in anger and frustration "Hey, that's my cab!" in the heaviest accent I have ever heard. The dazzling lights were captivating. They covered every corner, shining a bright red, green, and white. Beside me stood a store with a big neon sign that read *MERRY CHRISTMAS* hanging on its window. I watched the people inside invade each other's personal space. The store was not big but it was surely a crowd favorite. No one was able to move without bumping into someone. I've read about Christmas before in one of the many books we have in our library back home but witnessing it in person was breathtaking. It wasn't until I heard someone whisper "What is she wearing?" that I snapped out of my trance. I stared at myself in the reflection wondering what was wrong with what I was wearing. I didn't realize how out of place I looked compared to everyone else. I was wearing my favorite bright yellow dress that showed just enough cleavage that wouldn't bring my papi over the edge when he saw me in it. The dress was tailored just for me and had two slits made on both sides to show off one of my favorite assets: my beautiful tan thick thighs that were courtesy of my Mami. My hair was down, my curls perfectly framing my face. The silver hairpins in them make my olive skin pop. I loved how I looked but after I noticed the glares and whispers it was all I could focus on. I had ducked into the nearest empty alley and snapped my fingers for a wardrobe change. I now looked more like one of them, bundled up in a heavy dark brown coat lined in fur and matching earmuffs. I wanted to explore more without causing any more attention.

After seeing the beauty humans called Christmas, I made it a point to go back to the mortal realm at least once a month to see how their seasons changed. I started keeping a secret diary, cataloging my adventures in the human world. I would always find my way back to that same store. The same store where I saw the Merry Christmas sign. Their sign constantly changes with the seasons: *Happy Easter, Happy Valentine's Day,* and *Happy Saint Patrick's Day.* Whenever a new sign was hung, I would write it down to find its significance as soon as I got home. I swore one day I would walk inside and ask its owner the question that nagged at me every time I saw a new sign, *"Why does every holiday sign have to start with the word Happy?"*

The more I studied the human realm the more I adored it. Of course, it was far from perfect; let's face it the fae world also has flaws, but everything here seemed more simple. It would be simpler than any life that I would have in Aebriera that's for sure. I walked through the portal with my bags in hand. I knew it was wrong but I smiled. A sense of calm and relief washed over me, replacing the crippling anxiety that made my chest heavy. Where many faes would hate to be is now my paradise, my safety net. Am I upset about my situation? Yes. Did I run like a coward rather than face my impending coronation? Ab-so-fucking-lutely! I don't regret my decision. I've done what my parents have wanted my whole life and now it's my turn to do what I want. I'm not proud of it but I did what needed to be done. My parents and my people don't know it, but I just saved the Shadow Court from centuries of being miserable with me being their queen.

Chapter Three

So, I like to think of myself as being pretty wise, but as I stand in the middle of this alleyway with the portal behind me I realize that I haven't thought this whole plan through. I'm a stranger in a foreign land with no allies and nowhere to go. Sure, I've researched on humans and how they live but, what I hadn't asked - *how was I to make my way here?* I've never had a job or needed any currency to have a roof over my head or food in my stomach. I can't rely too much on my magic here, to ensure I don't raise any awareness of my presence. My blocking spell is airtight, if it's one thing I'm sure of is in my abilities to cast spells, I could cast this one in my sleep. Though it's easy to cast it's still a bitch due to the amount of power it drains and concentration it takes to try to shield my father out. It was one of the first spells my parents taught me and with good reason.

"There will be people that will want to hurt you, this will keep you safe if you need to stay hidden. Only use it in an emergency. When you cast this spell even we can't find you. It's not impossible to break but a lot of magic and willpower is required. The more you use your magic under this spell the more likely someone can find you." Mami and Papi told me. I nodded, agreeing to our verbal contract to never use it unless necessary.

I was too young at the time to understand why anyone would want to cause someone else harm, especially a child. As I grew up I learned just how evil faes could be and how many would grab me in the hopes it would ruin my papi. None had ever been brave enough to try. As I stood in the alleyway, hungry and trying to think of a solution to my housing problem, it hit me that I was officially alone.

I was used to having no friends back home, due to the glamorous life of homeschooling and being feared because of who my Papi was, but I have never been without my family. I wondered if the complete loneliness would break me while I was here. I hope I'll be as mentally strong as I am physically. At least I packed some of my comfort reads, they'll keep me company. I wondered if they noticed that I was missing yet. Probably not. Knowing them they think I am in my room sobbing over their news. Knowing Mami she will leave me be, no knocking on my door, just placing a plate of food at my door hoping that I will get up eventually and want to eat. She was never the consoling type. Papi would be the one to pick up the broken pieces while she would tell me to suck it up. The growling of my stomach brought me back to reality. How is it that my brain thought to pack books yet forgot to pack food? I should reflect on my priorities while I'm here.

With another grumble escaping from my stomach, I began my quest for food, but not before glancing into the display window of my favorite shop. There was no celebratory sign on the window, in its place was a *Help Wanted* sign. It seems today wasn't the day that I would walk inside and ask its owner about the happy signs but instead ask them about the help wanted sign and beg them for a job.

A bell chimed as the entrance door of the shop opened. As soon as you enter the store you're smacked in the face with the most delicious scent of freshly baked goods. Towards the front of the store is an abundance of clothing and mini statues. Though my eyes wanted to wander, my nose followed the amazing aroma. My feet dragged me to the back of the shop where a glass case stood full of different treats that made my mouth immediately salivate. Just as I finished wiping off the drool from the side of my mouth, the back door swung open.

"Wow." The words fell out of my mouth the moment I saw him. I almost broke my neck looking up at him. He had beautiful olive skin, brown shoulder-length hair that perfectly framed his green eyes, and a beard that called to me. I wanted to reach out and touch it.

I wonder if it feels as scruffy as it looks.

His arms were covered in black ink. I swore I saw a dragon's wing under his shirt sleeve. Though most of his art was covered, what I could see was beautiful. It complimented the muscles underneath. I found myself gravitating towards him, I could feel a pull coming from my core, as though I had found my center of gravity. Was this magic? It couldn't be. As I observed him, I could tell he was just an ordinary human.

A hot human that's making my whole body tingle without saying a single word.

I redirected my eyes to focus on the woman who was entering next to him. Her long red hair complimented her fair skin which was painted in freckles and bright blue eyes. I could feel the positivity seeping through her pores. While the man towered over me she wasn't even half my height. If I didn't know better I would think she was fae but as she tucked her hair behind her ear, there wasn't a pointed ear in sight. I adjusted my hair to make sure my ears were covered. I know I will have to glamour them away but I wasn't ready to let go of that part of my identity yet. My wild curly hair was always down anyway. I like to think of it as a curtain to hide from the world when the world becomes too much to handle, which I especially need for days like today.

Her blue eyes caught mine as she gave me a warm smile, inviting me to come closer for a conversation. I walked towards her, silently accepting her invitation as I mentally rehearsed my introduction.

"Hello and welcome to Holly's gifts and more! My name is Holly. How can I help you?" Her voice sounded just as I expected it to, sweet.

It took me a while to register the name of the store, the countless times that I've looked inside the glass window of this place never once did I bother to look at the name of the shop.

"Hi, my name is Corvina. No, it's Morticia. No that's a lie my first name is Corvina but please call me Morticia."

Oh my Gods why am I so socially awkward? Can the world just open up and swallow me whole, I think I can make that happen.

I looked at Mr. Tall, dark and mysterious, waiting for him to introduce himself but it never came. Instead, I received a side smirk that made my palms sweat.

"Okay well hello Corvina not Corvina but Morticia. How can I help you?" Holly placed a box that she was carrying on the counter.

"I didn't come in looking for anything in particular. It seems my nose has a mind of its own and I found myself in front of all these pastries. Did you bake these?" I inspected everything behind the glass, but the cookies caught my eye. I silently hoped that my drooling was under control. She took one out of the display case and handed it to me.

Both Holly and the tall man chuckled. He finally spoke and his voice sounded how velvet feels. "Oh, she wishes she did."

Holly slapped him hard on his bicep, he didn't even flinch. Suddenly it felt like my skin was on fire and I wanted to rip off the orange long-sleeve shirt that clung to my body.

"I can't bake to save my life, which is why Dante makes a great business partner." She smiled.

Dante, what's your story, and what about you has me acting like a fool?

"Oh is that all I am to you little sister?" he said as he rubbed the top of her head, messing up her hair.

Siblings. Hmm, interesting how two people can be opposites yet come from the same womb.

"Dante, what did I say about calling me little sister in front of customers? It takes away my authority as owner of this fine establishment!" She scowled at him as I held in a laugh.

"Well go ahead and eat the cookie, look at it any longer it's going to go stale." She nudged the cookie towards my mouth. I was so hungry I had no will to fight her so I took my first bite.

My eyes closed as they took it upon themselves to roll to the back of my head. I moaned in delight. I could be embarrassed about that later. I was starving and this cookie was even better than some of the treats we have back home.

"Music to my ears," Dante said in a sultry voice.

"Wow this is the best cookie I've ever had, and I'm not just saying that because it's the first thing I've eaten in hours." I wiped the crumbs from my mouth.

"How much do I owe you for this? I don't have much." I was rummaging through my pockets even though I knew I didn't possess any human currency.

Dante started walking in my direction, handing me a napkin to clean off the chocolate I'm sure was on my face. As I grabbed it from him, I couldn't help but notice the veins in his hands. Since when did I find veins in a man's hands attractive? Apparently, since today.

"I'm just the business partner, take it up with little Miss Big Boss over here," he said as he patted my shoulder.

As our skin touched, a wave of electricity passed through us, making us flinch. He walked away and I lost him in the sea of people in the store. Holly cleared her throat.

"Don't worry about the cookie, first one's on the house."

I just smiled and nodded, still unable to gather the courage to ask her for a job.

"I'm sorry if my brother scared you, he tends to intimidate people. Dante can be a little grumpy and unapproachable. He's what some people call a dark soul."

If only she knew what true darkness looked like, she would think Dante's personality was unicorns and rainbows.

"I wouldn't say he scares me, more like he's intriguing." My eyes wander as I speak to her, searching for him in the crowd.

I wanted to smack myself in the face the moment I said it.

Idiot! Did you tell Holly that her brother intrigues you?

You might as well wear a sign that says 'Hey I have the hots for your broody brother.' She's never going to hire me now. I might be an only child but I know that no one likes when someone is interested in their sibling.

You could see that shock in her face. "Well, that sure is a first." She kept working on organizing the baked goods.

How could that be a first? I mean look at him! How is it that no one else found him intriguing? Female humans must be blind or easily intimidated. Two things that I am not.

Pushing my thoughts about Dante to the side, I decided to go for it. The worst that could happen is that she says no when I beg her for the job.

"I couldn't help but notice the help wanted sign in your window, does complimenting the baker and not being scared of him earn me bonus points if I wanted the job?" She froze in place, scanning me as if she were trying to figure out if I was being sincere.

She was taking too long to reply for my liking and her silence was killing me.

"I'll be honest with you. I've never had a job before but I am a fast learner, I love the cookies, but I won't try to steal any to eat while I'm on the job I swear and I'll be on time."

Holly waved her hands at me to slow down. "Whoa, you're talking a mile a minute Morticia. Our sign has been up for so long due to Dante's lack of people skills. I'm shocked you want to work here. Are you new to the city?"

"Yeah, I'm from out of town. It's my first day here." I coughed nervously.

"Welcome to New York, Morticia. I'm all about giving chances and I won't lie to you. The fact you're not of Dante is a bonus. The job is yours." She reached her hand out but I ignored it, jumping to hug her instead.

I could kiss this woman right now. Of course, I won't because she's my new boss. Instead, I hugged her. I released her from my grasp, hoping that I didn't smother her to death with my excitement and gratitude.

"Thank you so much. I won't let you down. I swear to all the Gods." She looked at me oddly and I realized what I just said.

I've read that some humans believe in one god and some don't even believe there is one, I wonder what Holly believed in.

She brushed off my comment. "You start tomorrow at 11:00 am when the store opens."

I nodded in agreement. As I made my way to leave the store Holly called back out to me.

"Morticia! The cookies are always free for employees and I bet Dante would be even happy to bake you a personal batch." She gave a side-eyed glance towards the right side of the store.

My eyes followed hers and there he was. Dante was completely ignoring a customer as he stared at me. I said my goodbyes to Holly, knowing that he was still watching, I couldn't help but put a little more sway in my hips as I walked out the door.

Chapter Four

I walked out of the store with my head held high, proud that I successfully problem-solved. Now all I have to do is to be as lucky with finding a roof over my head, at least for the night. I could influence a human to let me rent a place but there's always a risk that using my magic could ping my location to those who were surely looking for me by now. Would it be worth the risk? Before I weighed the pros and cons, a sharp pain in my head stopped me in my tracks. The pain was so ferocious it completely paralyzed me.

I've never been on the receiving end of Papi's powers and holy shit this is painful. Papi has many powers, one being the ability to communicate telepathically. I was naive to think that his power wouldn't work between realms. No wonder why no one dared cross him. Though my blocking spell is perfectly intact, it's doing nothing to numb the pain as he tries his hardest to get through. He might be sick but I'm sure his wrath is just as deadly as ever. I've never defied my parents before, so they've never had to worry about me having a rebellious phase. My running away is completely out of character.

I knew that they would start a war with every court, thinking that I was taken instead of leaving of my own free will. It's why I left a goodbye note on top of the black vanity in my room. I didn't want them to start wars for no reason, even though my mother would be happy to pick a fight. My note was short but to the point.

I can't be what you want me to be. Please don't look for me. Te amo.

As I wrote that note I knew it wouldn't stop them from looking for me, that they would defy my plea but I did not anticipate this pain. It was getting more intense and all I could do was ride it out.

My body doubled over on the sidewalk as I waited for him to give up, for the pain to end; it just kept intensifying instead. My hands cradled my head as I tried soothing myself. I started to taste blood as I bit into my bottom lip, trying not to screech out in pain. Somehow I found the strength to duck into an alleyway before my legs gave out. I crawled towards a dumpster, laying in a fetal position while praying to the Gods that the pain would stop. A loud thud caught my attention. The bags I had been carrying were now next to me and alongside them was Dante, who was now standing over me. Another wave of pain hit me and this time I couldn't hold in my screams.

"Are you okay?" he asked on one knee.

I couldn't speak. I just kept cradling my head. He removed my hands and replaced them with his own. Just like that, I could feel my Papis' powers withdrawing as Dante cradled my face. Instant relief, no sharp pain, no wanting to cut my head off of my body. There was a sense of calm as if his touch was the cure. The embarrassment of him seeing me like this hit me and I stood up so fast that he almost toppled over.

"A decent person would say 'Thank you for checking that I wasn't dying.' This is why I stay away from people." He shook his head as he lifted himself off of the floor.

Is he aware that his touch helped take away the pain? Am I being crazy for suddenly being so suspicious of him or are my instincts telling me to stay away from this man? I brushed my worries to the side. Right now all I want to do is hug him for saving me from that pain. I decided against it. I didn't know this man, yet why do I ignore my qualms? Why does he feel so safe and familiar? I shouldn't be thinking about touching him let alone throwing my arms around his toned torso.

"I forgot my manners. I'm sorry, thank you." My voice came out hoarse.

His eyes were a combination of annoyance and impatience.

"Well, it took you long enough to remember them. You're welcome." He gathered all of my belongings from the floor.

Cabrón.

"Are you good to go? I have to get back to the shop."

"Yeah, I just have to figure out where I'm going."

"Are you lost?"

"Not exactly."

"You're not a runaway kid, are you? Please tell me that I'm not helping a minor escape the clutches of her unfair parents." He ran his palm across his face.

He wasn't too off about the runaway or the parents, but a kid. Did I really look that young? I looked down at my clothing and could see the confusion my outfit gave off. An oversized hoodie that showed none of my womanly shape and torn jeans. Note to self, get more adult-looking clothes.

"I'm far from a child, I'm a grown-ass adult. I don't have anywhere to go. I'm not from here and your sister was gracious enough to offer me a job but I'm still working on the boarding situation." I held my hand out gesturing for him to hand me my bags but he refused.

"You don't have any family you can stay with?" he asked as he scanned me with his eyes from head to toe.

There was no way that I was going to explain my family situation.

"If you're just going to harass me about my family life then you can just drop my things and I can move on with my day." I rolled my eyes.

There's that look of annoyance again. "Okay, Ms. Snippy. Reminder to self, don't bring up family." He looked as though he was having a mental war with himself. Dante growled before swinging my bag over his shoulder.

"Follow me." He started walking away, not allowing me a chance to respond if I was going with him.

I would be a fool to follow a stranger anywhere, yet here I am doing exactly that. He led us back into the shop. I caught a glimpse of Holly and she looked just as confused as I was. I followed him through the back door and up a spiral staircase, where we were greeted by a bright red door.

"After you." He held the door open for me to enter, as I did I saw beautiful exposed brick walls covered in art.

Paintings were hung in every corner. I found myself staring at a painting of dogs playing a card game.

So this is what humans considered art? Bizarre.

I was observing every inch of the place when Dante started to speak.

"It's not much but I think it's better than being on the street." He closed the door behind him, placing my bags on a black leather couch.

My fingers grazed the couch on my walk over to the kitchen. The kitchen had appliances that looked brand new, barely touched. I was never much of a cook, no matter how much my mother tried to teach me the family recipes. We had cooks at the manor back home but when it came to family meals she refused to share the recipes. She would give the cooks the night off as she took over the kitchen and threatened any who dared enter. This is what earned her the nickname Dramatica. The cabinets were see-through, though there wasn't much to see. There was, however, an abundance of wine glasses, each one a different shape and size. I turned and came face to face with a huge wine rack on the other side of the kitchen wall. The rack covered the wall from top to bottom full of wines from places I've read about in books and always wanted to visit. As I touched the bottles I read them out loud: "Italy, France, Portugal, Chile."

"Do you drink wine?" Dante's question took me out of my trance.

I could feel his breath on my neck. My mother always taught me to keep my defenses up, especially in unfamiliar territory, yet here I was with no guard up and feeling butterflies from a man being so close to my neck. What a great warrior I turned out to be, easily seduced by a man with a collection of wine and an attitude problem. If Mami could see me now, she would murder me herself. I nodded, scared that my voice would crack if I spoke. He took my hand off of the bottles as though I was a child who easily breaks fragile things.

"This is my collection, I've gone to all of these places and hand-picked each one myself. You can look, can carefully touch, but do not even think about drinking a drop of any of these." His voice came out stern and authoritative.

"What happens if I do?" I challenged him.

"Fuck around and find out. I dare you." He turned around exiting the kitchen.

"I'm not scared of you, Pendejo." I silently thanked the Gods my voice came out without any cracks.

"You should be."

I ignored his threat, continuing to study my surroundings.

"I don't speak Spanish but I've been called that word enough to know what it means."

"Good, I'll make sure to use it often then. Is this your apartment?"

"I haven't lived here for a while. I like to call it my escape room for when Holly is being, well... too Holly for my liking. No one has a key for this place but me and if I let you stay here I would appreciate it just being you." He stopped by the only closed door in the apartment.

I wanted to tell him he didn't have to worry, I had no plans on making friends or any interest in taking anyone to bed. That was the last thing on my mind. I checked out the small dining area. The table was a dark shade of wood and the chair seats were dark brown leather. One look at those chairs and I knew my thighs would no doubt stick to them on a hot summer day. I walked back into the living room, browsing an enormous bookshelf. My fingers touched all the spines as I read the titles of the books, keeping score of which ones I had access to back home.

"Are you always so quick to touch things that don't belong to you?" he snipped at me.

"Are you always so quick to give women you barely know access to your old apartment?" I raised an eyebrow at him.

I might be sweet, but I can be snarky if he's going to be an ass. It was a genuine question though. He's clearly not a people person so why go out of his way to help me, a complete stranger? I could tell he was fighting not to smile at my comment and I went back to admiring the books that covered every inch of the wall.

My question was quickly ignored. "I'll let Holly know that you'll be staying here and I'll give you a copy of the key tomorrow morning."

"A copy? So you'll still have access?" My throat went dry at the thought of him coming and going as he pleased.

"Who else will make sure my inventory goes untouched?" he said as he walked through the front door, slamming it shut behind him so hard that all the wine bottles shook.

"Pendejo," I yelled out, hoping he would hear me.

Chapter Five

Sleep did not come easy. I spent the night on the couch, I tried everything but couldn't get comfortable in his bed. My mind was filled with nightmares—a collage of different scenes of what looked like a war. I saw Papi commanding his army and Mami using her sword to decapitate whoever dared to cross her path. They all froze when they saw a bright white light approaching them from over the hilltops. Pure fear consumed their eyes. A shadowy figure began to emerge from the white light, something about them felt familiar, as if I knew the person who was about to slaughter everyone and everything that lay before them.

I awoke in a sweat, my curls frizzy and stuck to my drenched face. My breathing was erratic as I threw my blanket off and tried to steady my breathing. I looked towards the clock, 3:00 am. I decided against trying to go back to sleep. My mind was racing, reflecting on the events that happened during the past twenty-four hours. I was grateful that Papi hadn't tried to contact me again. It does make me worry if it's because his condition has worsened, maybe his power is growing weak.

I walked to the kitchen to grab a glass of water. It's still odd to me, to have to do little tasks like this without the assistance of magic. In time I'm sure I will get used to it. I opened the fridge, hoping to find any source of subsistence, to find its inside contents to be just beer.

So I'll starve but at least I'll have a great buzz.

He said I couldn't touch the wine but said nothing about the beer. I placed my water aside and cracked the beer open with my teeth. My mouth puckered as I took my first sip. This beer is crap compared to what we have back home. I hope this isn't a reflection of all the alcohol this realm has to offer. If so I'll have to stay sober for the remainder of my stay here and I'm not a fan of that idea.

I watched as the beer circled down the sink drain. I don't think I have it in me to fall victim to my dreams again so I made my way towards the bookshelves. There were books about many topics but a particular set caught my eye. They were in a box set and as I pulled it out of its case I read all the titles. *Fifty Shades of Grey, Fifty Shades Darker, Fifty Shades Freed.* I skimmed through the first one and blushed when I caught the words 'seduction' and 'bite' in them. Suddenly the room became hot as I pictured Dante in this apartment, reading these. I wonder if he physically went to the store to get them or had Holly do it for him out of shame. Male faes frown upon romance books, saying it's not real literature. I don't see them complaining when we use what we learn in the bedroom.

"Fuck it. Let's see what this Pendejo has been reading shall we." I told myself as I pulled the book off the shelf and started chapter one.

All of a sudden I woke up to a loud bang coming from the front door. I lunged towards my bags to grab my blade. I watched as the doorknob turned, crouching down to pounce and attack the intruder. I quickly hid my dagger once I realized it was Dante entering.

"You're late! How are you late if you sleep above where you work?" He rolled his eyes as he headed straight towards the kitchen.

I looked at the clock; noon. "Crap!" I scrambled to get a change of clothes.

He eyed his wine collection, making sure all was in order. He opened the fridge to grab a beer. I smirked when I saw him opening the beer bottle in the same manner as I did. My smirk transformed into a grimace as he acknowledged the empty bottle in the sink and opened his mouth.

"Did you drink a beer?" he asked, waving the empty bottle by his face.

"Look who's observant. I took one sip and then dumped it. You know what we call that in Spanish, mierda. How can you stand to drink that?" I walked towards the bathroom to change.

"I can drink it because it's mine to drink. I have great taste so you're delusional if you think this tastes like crap," he yelled to make sure I could hear him through the bathroom door.

"For someone who says they don't speak Spanish, you're sure understanding quite a few of the words I'm throwing at you."

"A lady called me a 'comer mierda' once so I looked it up. Not a nice thing to call someone by the way!"

"I'm sure you deserved it. I hope I get to meet her someday." I chuckled.

Dante stayed quiet.

"You took inventory, everything is intact so stop nagging me over some shitty beer. If you think you have great taste in beer, maybe it's a good thing I didn't touch your collection because I would hate to see how your taste in beer compares to your taste in wine." I wiggled on my jeans and threw on my top.

I swung open the bathroom door, slamming into Dante's hard chest. He towered over me, one hand on the door frame and the other gripping his beer. He swung his head over towards the disheveled-looking couch.

"Did you sleep on the couch?" His eyebrows scrunched together.

"I wouldn't call what I did sleeping. It was more like long blinks."

"Was there something wrong with the bed? Is it not to your liking, Princesa?"

Why did I get all tingly from him talking to me in Spanish? Oh no, Corvina get it together.

"Do not call me that."

"Come on, you're a little impressed by that. I even rolled my r."

Impressed, no. Aroused, yes.

I ignored his comment, going back to the topic at hand. "The truth is I didn't feel comfortable sleeping in your bed."

"It's a good bed. Don't sleep on the couch, it'll ruin the leather."

"Maybe later today you can give me a list of the do's and don'ts of staying at *Casa de Dante*."

He rolled his eyes, a hint of playfulness in them and a smirk emerged on his face, as though an evil idea had just entered his brain.

"Here," he said as he threw something at me.

I immediately regretted catching it because the damn thing stabbed me. I dropped it as soon as it pricked me and saw the blood coming out from the palm of my hand.

"Shit. I thought it was closed, it's your name tag." His hand nervously brushed through his hair.

I ran to the kitchen to rinse my hand off while Dante disappeared into the bathroom. You'd think the Gods would've blessed my kind with thicker skin so we wouldn't bleed so easily. Thankfully we do have amazing healing abilities so my cut was already gone by the time I rinsed my blood off. Dante returned from the bathroom with a red box with a white cross on its lid. He opened it and motioned for me to give him my hand.

"No need, I'm fine." I walked away from the sink and he grabbed my hand, stopping me from leaving the kitchen.

"There's blood, let me put a band-aid on it." He looked at my hand with squinted eyes trying to look for the puncture wound that was there just seconds ago.

I pulled my hand away from him, trying to act disgusted by his touch. This was now the third time that Dante and I had made physical contact and once again his touch brought goosebumps to my skin.

"You're making me more late than I already am. I'm going downstairs. You know your way out." I felt his eyes staring at me like daggers.

I should be more careful how I speak to the man who's giving me a place to stay but the feeling of putting him in his place is too good to give up.

Chapter Six

"I am so sorry again for being late." I apologized during my whole eight-hour shift to Holly and each time she kept saying, "It's fine Morticia, things like this happen." Once again, I could kiss this woman for being so kind.

I didn't expect to be overwhelmed by what Holly was teaching me. Holly was patient and kind as she went through everything I needed to know. I learned that those orange stickers on the clothing and mini statues are price tags. Their purpose is to indicate how much people pay for the items. I also learned how to use an item called the cash register, that's where the humans store the money made for those items. I must say, the currency of the mortal realm was very underwhelming to look at. I would love to question the person who decided green was a great color for money. One attribute I admired about Holly is that she didn't ask many questions. She never looked at me strangely when I needed help counting back change or learning the value of the ugly pieces of green paper. I'm sure she was just trying to be polite. Along with learning about cash I also had to learn about these objects called credit cards. It boggles my mind how humans found a way to use plastic as a form of currency, impressive if you ask me.

Dante didn't speak to me for the entirety of my shift, even

when we made eye contact as we snuck glances at each other. I didn't dare start a conversation with him, not when I couldn't explain a cut on my hand just disappearing if he decided to ask.

"Earth to Morticia!" Holly waved her hands in front of my face.

"Sorry, what were you saying about the system?"

"Sometimes it can freeze on us so you will just have to reboot it and if that doesn't work then you have to calculate the tax manually and just accept cash."

"Got it!"

What the hell is tax?

"I know this is horrible timing but I have to leave the city tomorrow to run some errands for the store so Dante is going to continue your training for the next couple of weeks."

Oh fun. I faked a smile and told her it wouldn't be a problem.

"You're free for the rest of the day. Do you have any plans?"

I shook my head no in response.

"Would you like to go out to dinner? My treat!" Holly grabbed cash out of the drawer, fanning herself with the money.

"Yeah, of course!" I chuckled at her, as she squealed in excitement.

"Perfect. Let me finish up here and we can head out."

I've never had a close girlfriend before. All the females back home were too intimidated to approach me and when I tried I just made a fool of myself.

"Can I ask you a question, Morticia?"

No.

No is what I wanted to say because I was scared of what was coming after that sentence. Instead what came out of my mouth was...

"Of course," I said, wanting to bite my nails off their beds from nerves.

"Where are you from?"

Mierda.

"No place you would know of."

She just nodded, taking the hint that was all the information she was getting out of me.

"Sorry if my question made you uncomfortable. I forget that not everyone is an open book. Stay right here, I'll be right back."

I broke my no-magic rule, watching her whispering to Dante was too much for me to handle. I had to know what she was saying to Dante, make sure that I didn't just fuck all of this up by refusing to share a part of myself with her.

"What are your thoughts on Corvina?" Holly asked.

"I think it's weird she likes to go by her middle name and pretends her first name doesn't exist but she's fine I guess. I don't have an opinion, I haven't talked to her much." Dante continued rolling his dough as he talked, avoiding eye contact with Holly.

"A name preference is nothing to be alarmed about. Strange you don't have an opinion since you gave her a place to stay. Rent-free, I might add. You haven't let anyone stay there since..."

Dante immediately froze, slowly turning his head towards Holly and giving her a stare that would make death himself stop in its tracks. So Holly did, she stopped whatever she almost dug up from his past.

"Holly, she just needed a place to stay. Would you have preferred if I looked the other way? Mom and Dad taught us better than that. I might not have rainbows and unicorns flying out of my mouth when I speak like you do, but I'm not completely heartless."

"Yes Dante, I know the mantra. Never heartless, always an asshole." She rolled her eyes.

"I'm glad you remember, now don't you have something better to do than watch me roll out this dough?" He glanced my way.

"I do. I have a dinner date with your tenant. Don't wait up." Holly went on her tiptoes to kiss Dante on the cheek.

Dante's eyes stayed glued onto mine. I quickly pretended to organize some clothing on the rack beside me.

"Even assholes need love too," Holly whispered in Dante's ear as she walked away.

Chapter Seven

Holly is a talker and I was thankful for that. Dinner would've been awfully quiet otherwise. It was a short walk from the store to the Italian restaurant Holly picked. The nerves I had slowly melted away; Holly has a way of making people feel at ease. We talked about a plethora of different topics. We both had ordered pasta with a glass of wine. Our wine came first and Holly took a sip before she spoke.

"I want to ask you something but I feel like if I do I'm going to scare you away."

"It's not like you don't know where to find me." I chuckled before taking a sip.

This wine was much better than that beer back at the apartment. Thank the Gods I can at least have wine while I'm here.

"Touche," she said before taking a deep breath.

"Do you not have any family? I'm sorry if that sounded insensitive I honestly don't know how else to ask that question."

Crap.

"No, you're fine. Family is just a complicated subject for me."

Think, Corvina. Think!

"I'm an orphan. I have zero contact with my family."

That's not a complete lie.

"Okay, that's a good enough answer for me."

"No follow-up questions?"

Why would you ask her that? Estúpida!

"You're going to find that I'm a complex person Morticia. I'm high-strung, bossy, and sassy. Dante likes to call me 'hell on heels' and he's not wrong. I'm all those things but I'm also respectful of other people. If that's all you want to tell me then that's fine by me."

Our plates of pasta came to the table and I smiled at Holly, silently thanking her for understanding. Both plates of pasta were delicious, even though most of the sauce from my pasta landed on top of the red and white checkered tablecloth. I was scarfing down the rest of my pasta when Holly asked another question that had me choking.

"Is there a special someone in your life?" she sipped on her white wine.

I choked on the noodle I was slurping down and Holly chuckled as I saved myself by chugging some wine.

"No. I'm not really looking for love. I've tried it once and it failed, miserably might I add. I think I'm better off without it."

"That's crazy talk. No one is better off without love. Love is what makes life worth living. A life without love is nothing but sadness."

I scoffed. "Are you sure about that? Because all I've gotten from love is nothing but sadness."

"Well, that's a load of crap. There was a time when love made you blissful. A time when the mere mention of their name sent butterflies to your stomach. A love that consumed you to the point that you felt empty without it, without that person around. Just because that love ended doesn't mean you should damn the love that is to come. Invite love in Morticia." She finished off her wine with a smile on her face.

"We can add hopeless romantic to the list of things you mentioned earlier."

"Damn right you can and I'm not ashamed of it."

I stayed quiet, pondering the words she spoke so eloquently. My heart tugged at me, trying to confirm her words as true. I would never admit it to her.

"I have a sneaking suspicion that you've given this speech multiple times before," I questioned her, the guilt was instantly written on her face.

"Well when you have Dante as a brother, you give quite a few speeches. This might be one of the many." We both laughed.

"Exactly how many times have you given him this love speech?"

"A few times after... someone left his life but that's not my story to tell." Holly fell quiet, sad as though that person also left a hole in her life.

"Well, what about a story you can tell? From how you talk about it, you must have a special someone who makes it... what is it you said? Oh yeah, blissful." My question made her blush.

"Yeah. I do, they're great. The best thing that's ever happened to me and they came right after my first love completely broke me. I'm meeting up with them after this."

"Oh don't let me hold you up. Let's go so you can get to your epic love."

She waived down our waiter to ask for our checks, fighting me as she told them one whole check instead of two separate ones.

"I have a feeling you and I are going to become the best of friends Morticia," Holly said as she signed her name on the dotted line.

"Now that's a love I won't deny. Your friendship will be all the love I need." I told her as I hugged her goodbye.

"We'll see about that."

Her phone rang and I couldn't help but smile at how giddy she became.

"Babe, I'm on my way and have leftover pasta." She winked at me before making her way down the street.

She looked like she was floating on air, as though the mere knowing that she was on her way to meet her love sent her flying. I felt a pain in my chest, wondering if I would ever feel that kind of love.

Chapter Eight

The next couple of weeks went by pretty quickly. Surprisingly Dante was a good trainer and only made snarky comments when we were off the clock. I just rolled my eyes in response and that was our routine. Teach, learn, snark, eye roll, repeat. Every now and again I would find him trying not to laugh at my comebacks by coughing.

"You know for someone who has a crappy taste in beer you have great taste in pizza," I said to him while on break together one afternoon.

It was the first pizza I've ever had but he didn't need to know that. There was grease everywhere and I'm sure it wasn't the healthiest thing to eat but I wasn't lying about how much I enjoyed it. I didn't have anything to compare it to, however, I didn't spit it out as soon as I took a bite so it passed.

"You're never going to let that beer thing go are you?" He rolled his eyes and took another bite of his pizza and a swig of the beer in question.

"Never. Should you be drinking alcohol while on your lunch break?" I smiled before demolishing the rest of my food.

"That's the beauty of being your own boss. You make the rules and yes, the rules say I can." He took another big swig of beer.

The one thing Dante didn't have to teach me was customer service. I was 'Very easy to talk to and approachable' according to the guest suggestion box in the store. All these years I just thought I was awkward, turns out these humans think it's charming! Dante and I would read them at the end of every shift. Whenever he would read something kind about me he would roll his eyes and pretend to gag.

Dante grabbed the box as I said farewell to our last customers and closed the front door.

"I can hear the praise now. 'Morticia was amazing. Morticia was so helpful and kind.'"

"I get it, you have a praise kink." Dante rolled his eyes as my cheeks reddened.

"If you don't just read those cards, Pendejo."

"Si, Princesa," Dante smirked, knowing I hated his nickname for me.

I'm an actual princess Cabrón and if you ever spoke to me like that on my territory you would've been killed by now.

Of course, the first card praised me so he pretended to choke on the water he was drinking. I grabbed the card from his grasp before he could spit water all over it.

"You should be glad that I'm liked and I'm not... what exactly did that card say about you?" He tried to grab the card from my hand but was unsuccessful.

"Oh yeah, 'Intimidating and unapproachable'." I mocked him and he wet his fingers with the water in his cup and flicked droplets at me.

"I don't care what they have to say about me as long as they keep coming for more of my desserts." He pointed at the empty dessert display case to make his point.

"Maybe you should tell them that you have no love in your

heart because all of it goes into your cookies." I took a bite of a sea salt double chocolate chip cookie I stashed away.

I always moaned when I ate one of his sweet treats. It started off pure joy for his baking but when I noticed that his lip would twitch up in a curved side smile every time I did it. Now I made it a point to react that way. It was the only time a smile threatened to escape his lips in my direction. We were almost finished reading all the cards when we both reached for the last one, our hands touched and my stomach dropped from the contact. We both recoiled our hands and I gestured for him to grab the last one to read it. As he read it to himself a flush of color came to his cheeks. I couldn't believe it, Dante was blushing.

"I'm not reading this out loud." He walked away, placing the card on the bench.

Dante made it to the kitchen by the time I grabbed the card and read it. You could tell from the handwriting it was written by a young kid.

"My mom is making me do this since she doesn't want to but is scared of telling that mean guy no. The store is nice I guess, my mom bought a lot of stuff. The girl who helped us is HOT! Hopefully, the grumpy guy doesn't run her away."

I chuckled as I walked my way toward the kitchen.

"Are you jealous, Dante?" I asked as I held the card between my index and middle finger.

"Oh please, get over yourself. So a kid thinks you're hot. When I was his age I thought *Lola Bunny* was hot."

"You thought a bunny rabbit was hot?" I questioned, not knowing who this bunny was, and made a mental note to look her up later.

"You've never seen *Looney Tunes* either? God the watch list for you keeps getting longer and longer."

"Anyway, I'm going to go take my hot self upstairs. Need help with anything before I go?"

"Nah, I'm good. You can take your hot ass to bed." Dante stopped what he was doing, and rosy cheeks again returned to his face.

"So, you do think I'm hot?" I smirked.

"I think you're a pain in my ass, now leave before I make up work for you to do." Dante put his fingers to his temple, rubbing them slowly in circles.

I walked away, debating whether to return the card to the pile. Though I completely agree with the kid's comment about me being hot stuff, his comment about Dante pushing me away could never be true. Honestly, I wish he would pin me against a wall while he cradles my face in his hands so I can feel that electricity I felt the first time he touched my shoulder. I thought about that shock more than I would ever admit to him. I think my reading of *Fifty Shades* is getting to my head. He barely wants to smile at me. I doubt he sees me as anything other than a woman who needed his help and took pity on. I shoved the card into my pocket, keeping it as a memento of the first time Dante had rosy cheeks in my presence.

Chapter Nine

I wish I could say that the nightmares stopped and that I was able to have a good night's rest but that would be a lie. Each night it becomes more vivid, yet I never see the mysterious entity hiding in the white light.

As I lay in bed, wondering how long I could survive without proper rest, a soft knock on the front door startled me. I waited a few more minutes, knowing Dante would appear since his idea of respecting my privacy was knocking once and then barging in.

Dante never showed. Instead, there was a second knock on the door. Dagger in hand I crept over to the front door. I swung the door open and immediately threw my dagger behind the door when I saw Holly's face.

"What was that noise?" Her eyebrows scrunched together.

"I didn't hear anything." I slid my foot, pushing my dagger behind the coat rack.

She shrugged her shoulders. Her smile was beaming as she shoved an array of shopping bags at me.

"I was hoping you were still around, did you miss me?" Holly twirled a piece of hair around her finger and pouted.

"What kind of question is that? Of course I did, after all, you did leave me with your brother."

"That's why I was hoping that you were still around." She chuckled.

"One of those bags is for you by the way. It's a cell phone. I found myself wanting to text you so consider this a welcome aboard gift." She pointed to the white bag.

"Thank you but now this means you're stuck with the task of teaching me how to use this thing." I inspected the box that held a cell phone inside. A mirror image of the one that Holly was always typing on and used to watch cat videos.

"No worries, it's easy. Even my grandmother knew how to use one. Bless her soul."

"Thanks. You'll be proud to hear that Dante did an excellent job training me."

"Oh honey, I was never worried about his training abilities. I was more worried about his people's abilities. I'm unsure if you've noticed, but he can be a bit standoffish."

I plastered a look of shock on my face as I gasped. "Dante, standoffish? NEVER!" We both busted out into laughter.

The hairs on the back of my neck stood up and a rush of heat ran through my body.

"Speaking of the devil, hello brother."

I turned around and there he was, leaning against the door frame looking dark and brooding as usual.

I've never felt intimidated by a man until now. My hair was a mess because I refused to wash it after my shift yesterday and I had on a pair of flannel pants with a tank top that said *Bonita Mode.* Kill me now. I tried to turn around before Dante got a good look at me.

"Hello sister, I hope Morticia didn't give you a key Holly because that would be breaking one of the rules."

I opened my mouth to respond but froze as Dante walked past

me and whispered "Nice pj's," in my ear.

Kill me now. I mean it. If the Gods are real, answer my plea.

I felt my skin turning red as he eyed me from the couch. My voice finally found its way back to me.

"Remind me again, where is that list, I still can't find it anywhere?" I glared at him.

"That's because you haven't bothered to look. Check the fridge door." His elbows rested on his knees as he sat relaxed on the couch.

I hate how much his muscles flexed as he sat there watching me. This distraction is not helping at all. I walked over to the fridge, burning up even more when I saw a list taped to its door. I crumbled the list without reading it and threw it at Dante's head. Little Pendejo dodged it. He gave me that stupid smug look that I love to hate.

"Will you two quit it? I don't have a key Dante, she let me in." Holly's voice was coated in annoyance.

"I swear if people saw you both bickering the way you do they would swear you two are the siblings."

Dante and I both replied with a harmonious "Ew."

Holly cleared her throat and began speaking as I retreated into the bedroom to change.

"Anyway. I'm ecstatic to see my store hasn't burned down and that my two employees are getting along. As best as they can anyway." She side-eyed Dante.

"You do remember I don't work for you right? I'm your partner!" Dante emphasized as I resurfaced from the bedroom.

Dante looked me up and down quickly before returning his attention to Holly.

What was that about?

"Okay, partner. I wanted to have a team meeting about the

annual bake-off."

What in the Gods is a bake-off?

Dante groaned and began to protest.

Holly cut him off. "I don't want to hear it! We have three months, there is no time to waste and I already signed the shop up. No take backs, come on Dante! We haven't entered in years because we haven't found anyone for you to enter with."

"We don't have to enter, there's no reason to anymore. That competition was to start a buzz about the store and get business. Business is booming, we don't need the extra promotion." Dante tried to reason with her but Holly wasn't budging.

She gave him a stern look. "Dante you know that's bull. There's no such thing as too much publicity. You used to have fun competing. I swear to God I saw you smile one year while competing! This is happening. You know the rules, it has to be a two-person team. Lord knows I don't have any business being in a kitchen so Morticia will join you."

"I've never baked anything in my life," I interjected.

"That's fine Dante's old partner was also clueless in the baking department and he trained her so well they won two years in a row. He'll teach you his ways; think of him as your Yoda."

"My what?" Dante and Holly looked at me in horror.

"You don't know *Star Wars*?" They both said in shock.

I just shook my head and added a mental note to look up whatever that meant.

Holly and Dante stared each other down as though they were having a personal telepathic conversation. Finally, Dante put his hands up in the air, surrendering to Holly. She jumped up and down gleefully, clapping her hands, excited about her victory.

"Fine. I'll teach her everything I know. No fucking around in my kitchen. A lot of my equipment is expensive so don't touch anything unless I teach you how to use it or tell you that you can touch it."

"Yay, more things I can't touch without your permission, how exciting." I rolled my eyes.

"I'm not excited about this either Princesa but our boss has given us a job to do so let's win this shit."

"Partner!" Holly corrected him.

"Oh, now you listen." He shook his head as he rolled his eyes at Holly.

Note to self: Find a way to hit Dante in the head with a rolling pin and make it look like an accident.

Chapter Ten

"You're doing that wrong." Dante's jaw was tense.

"I'm trying, can you give me one second for the love of Gods!" I yelled, throwing my hands in the air.

I was frantically trying to make sure that the first batch of cookies I did without Dante's help was perfect and I was failing. There was flour everywhere. My hair, my clothes, my apron, and even my shoes were covered in flour and I didn't even care how crazy I looked in front of Dante because I was overwhelmed. How did he make this look so easy? How is it that I'm able to beat someone's ass in hand-to-hand combat, wield a full-sized sword and summon powerful magic but I can't figure out how to successfully bake a damn cookie correctly? I should've thanked the chefs back home more than I did, especially the pastry team.

"Maldita sea!" I threw the rolling pin at the batch of dough I was working on and it rolled onto the floor.

No matter how hard I tried, the dough wouldn't become the right consistency. I kept throwing flour at it hoping that would fix it. Dante's constant sideline comments did nothing but add fuel to the fire that was my rage.

"I'm not sure what you just said and I know a rolling pin isn't super expensive but can you not throw shit around in my kitchen." Dante picked up the rolling pin.

"I said fuck this dough, fuck this bake-off, I quit." I stormed out as I untied my apron and threw it in the trash. If I never saw another cookie in my life that would be fine by me, even if it's as delicious as his are. I ran up the stairs to my apartment and even though it was pointless I still locked the front door. No footsteps echoed behind me and I was glad. Hopefully, he'll stay away. My therapist has tried for years to get me to control my fuse but right now none of the techniques she taught me are working. I'm just not used to being bad at anything. If Dante walks through that door right now, I won't hesitate to release my frustrations on him.

I winced in disgust as I looked into the bathroom mirror. My hair was wrecked and I had flour in places that you should never have flour. After 30 minutes of vigorous scrubbing in the shower and by the grace of the Gods, I felt clean enough to flop onto the couch. My eyes wandered over to the book on the counter, its gray tie cover calling to me and as I reached the halfway point there was a light knock on my door. I didn't move. I didn't bother to answer the door, knowing it was most likely the man who always left himself in. The sound of a second knock on the door filled the apartment. Maybe it wasn't Dante after all. I held my page of the book using the fairy bookmark I bought at the store. What can I say, I'm a fan of irony. I'm not, however, a fan of surprises. So when I opened the door to see Dante's eyes staring at me my heart skipped a beat.

The feeling of annoyance came bubbling back up to the surface as he stood there, leaning casually against the door frame.

"Look at you finally understanding how knocking works." I rolled my eyes leaving the door open behind me as I walked back towards the couch.

He stood quiet, the silence was killing me. This man makes me want to murder him every time he speaks. This should be a blessing from the Gods that he's quiet. So why am I anxiously waiting for him to say something, anything? The silence continued as he entered the kitchen, the only sound filling the silence being the pouring of liquid. Holly was nice enough to fill the fridge when she noticed all the takeout containers that filled up my trash. He stomped his way back to me, the sound of his boots made the air heavy as he sat beside me. I wanted to scream as soon as I saw what he placed on top of the table.

"Are you trying to feed me a batch of your fucking cookies right now? I feel inferior enough, I don't need you rubbing it in my face how good your cookies are compared to mine." I turned my back towards him, refusing to eat.

He nudged the plate closer to me and it took all of my strength not to throw it against the wall. The thought of the plate shattering and the cookies crumbling brought a smirk to my face. Though my impulsive thoughts were strong I fought them and kept ignoring the plate and Dante. Finally, the silence broke.

"If you don't just shove this damn cookie in your mouth already." He took a cookie off the plate and forcefully placed it in my hand.

"Well, look who has decided to talk. Thank you for gracing me with your voice. Now that you have, can you explain how dare you feed me your cookies after I failed miserably at baking mine? You want to gloat about how much better you are than me that badly?"

If only I could show him all the things I'm better at than him, like conjuring up a magical whip so I can bend him over, and... Dante broke my train of thought.

"Morticia I swear I will shove this cookie down your windpipe if you don't just eat it already."

I sucked my teeth. I would love to see him try, he would be on his back in seconds flat.

"Fine. You don't have to be so violent." Dante's head looked like it was about to explode.

The cookie was a mess in my hand, he had crushed it out of anger. I took a bite, hating that it was as delicious as I knew it would be.

"Is it to your liking, Princesa?"

I hate him.

"What kind of question is that? You already know how I feel about your cookies. It was delicious as usual." I took a sip from the glass of milk.

If my words could spit venom Dante would be screaming in pain. My ears began ringing as I heard a rich chuckle coming from Dante.

I just might claw his throat out.

This man gets under my skin in ways I didn't know were possible.

"Princesa, I could never forget how you feel about my cookies. I hate to break it to you but those aren't mine. This is the batch you abandoned earlier today." He took a bite of one of the cookies and grabbed the cup of milk from my hand, helping himself to a sip.

"You don't give yourself enough credit. You're not failing at baking, you're learning and growing. Stop trying to be perfect. You could never be me." He winked and I slapped his arm. He didn't even flinch.

"I've just never been bad at anything."

"Of course you haven't. Princesses can never be bad at

anything."

We can't afford to be, not when it can put our kingdom at stake.

"What's something you're good at?"

I glared at him and I almost fought him on the spot before he realized how his question came off.

"I'm genuinely curious, I'm not asking to be a 'Pendejo'." He placed air quotations over the word.

I fought a laugh, he tried with that one but the pronunciation was horrible.

My brain goes through them all, debating what hidden talents I could disclose to him.

"Fighting. Not verbal fighting but actual hand-to-hand combat. I took classes and beat every guy in the class."

It wasn't a complete lie.

"Poor, weak bastards. Well, I'm sure it took you a lot of practice to be that good so put that same energy into this."

"That took years to do. I don't have the luxury of time right now. Letting you and Holly down isn't an option." I eat when I'm nervous and my hand automatically reaches for another cookie.

"You won't, especially Holly. She's just happy we can compete again. What's that saying? When life gives you flour, bake a cake."

"That's a stupid saying."

"It's better than anything you're reading in there." He points to the *Fifty Shades of Grey*. Even though his words are full of judgment, his eyes reflect sadness as he looks at them.

"Hey, it's your book! You spent your hard-earned cookie money on it. It was the only book on your shelf that looked even remotely interesting and honestly, I'm learning a lot from it." I blushed.

"Oh yeah? What have you learned from it, Morticia?"

I'm unsure when it happened, but his face is now inches from mine. So close that I can smell the sweetness from the chocolate of the cookies on his breath. My teeth clamp down on my bottom lip as I try to stop myself from licking him, from seeing if it tastes as good as he smells. I cleared my throat, hoping that a response would come to me but nothing did.

"Think about it and you can tell me later." The bastard winked.

He walked towards the front door, leaving the plate of cookies on the living room table. "I'll see you tomorrow. There's more work to be done to get the cookies to Dante's level but I'll leave you to your sex book."

"It's your sex book, not mine!" I threw my half-eaten cookie at the back of his head.

The cookie hit him dead center and crumbled into pieces upon impact. Dante stopped, shaking his head to get the crumbs out of his hair before walking out the door.

I walked over to clean up my mess, hearing him mumble through the door.

"Princess has one hell of an arm." followed by his deep throaty laugh.

Chapter Eleven

Dante was staring me down, his green eyes darkening as he looked at me from across the room. I don't remember how we got into this staring contest but I know I didn't want to lose. Neither of us blinked, we were frozen like statues. I made the mistake of licking my lips, giving them the moisture they so desperately needed. Dante lunged forward, his large body now hovering over me. I didn't dare move. My body felt completely paralyzed from the waist down. It's by the grace of the Gods my body hadn't already collapsed. His breath mingled with mine as he spoke.

"How dare you look at me that way and lick your lips. You don't understand what that can do to a man, what it does to me." His hands left a trail of heat as they explored my body.

Dante's fingers felt like a flutter as they moved from my jaw to my waist, his eyes following his movements. My face heated as I saw the goosebumps forming on my skin, knowing he could see them too. My breathing was uneven, he placed his large hand on my chest as a reminder to breathe. My steady breathing didn't last for long. I gasped as he grabbed a handful of my ass. That caught his attention and his eyes were back on mine.

"I've wanted to do this since the first day I heard you moan after eating one of my cookies. I'm not a jealous man, but fuck, as stupid as it sounds I was jealous of that cookie." His thumb lightly grazed my bottom lip.

"I want nothing more than to be the only thing that makes you moan that way." He whispered in my ear.

Dante's lips were soft against my earlobe.

"Do you want me to make you moan Princesa?"

I couldn't help but shiver as I shook my head yes.

"I need to hear you say it." He kissed my neck, causing me to whimper.

"Please, Dante."

I've never been the type to beg a man for anything but for this, I would get on my knees. For Dante, I would beg and plead and move all the worlds to have him keep touching me this way.

The reply barely left my lips before he crushed them with his own. I could taste the hunger on his lips and melted at how soft they were on mine. His tongue slipped into my mouth and I moaned, hoping that I tasted as good to him as he did to me.

"That's my girl. The moan that is music to my ears." He wrapped one of his hands around my throat while the other slipped under my shirt and bra.

"More," I whispered.

"What do you want more of Morticia? Is it the praise that you want? I have no problem with that. I will praise you all night. Would you like that Princesa? Do you want me on my knees praising you?"

"Si," I begged.

"You're mine, Corvina Morticia Umbra." He growled in my ear.

I woke up not only short of breath but also with my underwear soaked. I wasn't sure if I was glad it was a dream or pissed that the dream was over but that's all it was, a dream. The clock on the nightstand read 7:00 am, right next to the clock was *Fifty Shades Darker* and I gave the middle finger to the book. I just *had* to continue the series.

I rolled out of bed and started the shower hoping that the cold water would help me forget about Dante but as I washed my body my fingers lingered just above the place that I knew would bring me the release I needed.

No.

I swatted my hand away.

I will not touch myself to the thought of that Pendejo.

The dream felt so real. I've heard of faes back home capable of constructing dreams so vivid that their actual bodies travel with them but I've never experienced that myself. I wonder if not using my powers as often as I did back home would cause my powers to want to escape. I wrapped myself in a towel collecting the sweaty sheets and throwing them inside the washer Holly was so kind to teach me how to use.

There was a knock on the door and before I could ask who it was the door flew open and as it did my towel fell to the ground, my whole naked body exposed. I ran and dove behind the couch leaving the towel in the middle of the floor.

"Rise and shine. We got shit to do, woman!" Dante screamed as he let himself in.

He stood staring at the towel on the floor and before I could completely lose my dignity I snapped my fingers to dress myself.

"What the hell are you doing on the floor? Get up and clean up this towel from the floor. I'm not letting you stay here to treat it like a pigsty." He walked over to the kitchen, taking his inventory per usual.

I've pondered if I should ever take a bottle as a joke and watch his reaction. That temptation almost won, to pick up a bottle and chug it. That temptation was the strongest on the days he pissed me off, which was just about every day. Today might be the day I go through with the plan.

"I thought you finally learned how to knock properly?" I rose from the floor, smoothing out the skirt I was now wearing.

"It was a one-time thing, sweetheart, don't get used to it."

I cringed at the word sweetheart and Dante noticed.

"Sorry, I meant Princesa. Is that better? Are you getting used to your little nickname?" Dante pinched my cheek. He swiftly moved his hand before I could bite it off.

He winked and butterflies started to flutter. Not the stomach kind but the kind that can be found centered in the lower half of my body. I took a deep breath, trying to clear my head and calm myself down before I used my powers to murder him. How can I find someone attractive but also want to unalive them? Someone make it make sense.

"You're going to want to get out of that skirt."

"You wish."

"Don't flatter yourself, it just isn't practical for what we're doing today."

"You do know that today is my day off right?" I yelled from my room as I changed into denim cargo pants.

I heard Dante munching on something as he said, "Just because you have a day off from the store doesn't mean you have a day off from me. We have research to do."

"Ever stop to think I might have other plans?" I walked over to retrieve my towel, tossing it on the couch.

"That doesn't belong there." He pointed at the towel placement.

"Just like your grubby little hands don't belong on my apple."

I grabbed the red apple out of his hand and took a bite.

"Morticia, there is nothing little about me." He snatched the apple back from my hand, sticking his tongue out at me before using it to lick all around the perimeter of the apple.

Why is that so hot when it's meant to gross me out?

"I know you don't have any plans because Holly is out with her girlfriend and she's your only friend."

"I'm sorry, her what?" I was confused.

I hate that he was right. Without Holly, I would have no other plans but it doesn't mean I want to spend a day off with Dante. On days I had off from the shop she would invite me out for lunch or shopping. We would talk about our interests. What books we were reading, and what Dante did to piss us off that day. Her significant other would pop up in conversation but never once did she mention her lover was a woman. Not that I cared about the gender of who she was seeing, I've taken on a female lover a time or two myself, but I would think it would pop up during conversation. Did it mean she didn't trust me enough? Did she think I would judge her?

"Oh shit. Did I just out my little sis? Dammit, please don't tell her I told you. I honestly thought you knew, you both are always gossiping. Isn't that what girls do? Gossip about love and shit." He pretends to gag.

"Excuse me, we are women, not girls. Also, fuck love, there's way more interesting things to talk about."

Dante gave me a puzzled look, as though this was the first time he'd ever heard a woman speak of love so negatively. His lips pursed, as though he was trying hard to keep it shut. He shook his head as though to shoo the question on his mind away.

"Don't worry I won't tell her. It hurts that she doesn't trust me enough to tell me." I toss on a jacket and motion Dante to move towards the front door.

"Don't take it personally, she doesn't tell people. I'm surprised she told me honestly but to be fair she did spill the beans when we were younger that I'm adopted."

Dante kept walking down the stairs as I came to a halt.

He stopped halfway down to look at me.

"Okay, from the look on your face, I can see I threw another truth bomb at you. Please don't look at me like I'm such a poor unwanted kid cause I won't have any of that bullshit around me. Now can you hurry your ass up, we're already running behind."

I had so many questions that needed answering but I decided now was not the time to push him.

"Where is it exactly that we're going?" I closed the door, rushing down the stairs to catch up to him.

I stood by him trying to catch my breath as he threw on his leather jacket.

"Like I said, we're doing research."

Chapter Twelve

"Absolutely not. Estás loco," I said as I looked at the contraption Dante was straddling.

"I've never had this type of reaction to Dragon before." The metal beast made some roaring noise and I jumped.

"You named it Dragon? That is the furthest thing from a dragon I've ever seen." I handed him his helmet and started my walk towards the shop.

Only the most elite of faes have dragons because they have a lot of upkeep. They're worth it because of their fierceness in battle and once you've bonded with one they are loyal to you for life. I've had my fair share of rides on them but I refuse to mount this one. I doubt that riding Dante's version of a dragon would be as peaceful as riding an actual dragon if only I could take him to experience what riding a true creature of flight is like. I remember the first time I took to the sky with one. The calm it brought me as the wind blew through my hair and the feeling of the dragon's heartbeat as it took flight. I used to ride all the time until the day that my favorite dragon passed, Vespera. I never bonded with her, I've heard there's a certain feeling you get when you do. Papi took her into battle and she never came back home. I was grateful for her sacrifice, that she protected him so he could return home to us, but it didn't make the pain of her death hurt any less.

"I swear I won't go as fast as I normally do. You'll have a helmet on, I promise it's perfectly safe. I've never been in a wreck before." He was holding out the helmet hoping his words changed my mind.

"None of your words are compelling me to do this. Can't we just walk?" I looked towards the perfectly safe sidewalk that was beside me.

"There's too much ground to cover and though I am the definition of physically fit, I really don't feel like walking through the whole city."

"Cocky much?" I crossed my arms across my chest.

"You haven't seen me naked, Princesa." Dante wiggled his eyebrows.

I haven't and I fear if I ever do it will be the death of me.

I didn't budge as I stood on the sidewalk, arms still wrapped around me.

Dante pinched the bridge of his nose, sighing heavily before he spoke.

"Morticia my mom used to ride this and that woman was scared of everything."

"I say this with all respect. I will not be joining her in the afterlife today. It's fine, you can complete your research and I'll watch the store. The store that you decided to close for the day without telling Holly I might add."

"Oh so you're not only a puss but you're a narc too?" He raised his eyebrow, arching it in a way that shouldn't be so attractive but dammit it was.

"That sentence made no sense to me but it doesn't matter. I'm going to open up the shop."

He yelled a sentence that stopped me in my tracks.

"What did you just say?"

"I said, 'If you ride with me I'll let you open one bottle of wine from my collection.' One of your choosing." He dangled the helmet at me as if I was a horse and the helmet was a carrot.

Gods be damned, he knew that was an offer I couldn't refuse. I walked over to him, aggressively grabbing the helmet from him as he gave me a devilish grin.

"This wine better be the best damn wine that I've had in my whole existence."

"How old are you again? Like twenty-eight? You haven't existed for long and trust me it will be."

He wasn't wrong. I look twenty-eight, but I've looked this way for a long time. I wonder if our age difference would creep him out.

"If I die you still need to open a bottle in my honor and pour some down my throat, my corpse will appreciate it. So help me if you don't, I'll haunt you for the rest of your life."

"Cross my heart and hope you don't die." His index and middle fingers interlocked as he made an 'x' motion across his chest where his heart was located.

How dare he look that damn good.

I smacked his arm before putting on the helmet. I knew there wasn't any way that a crash would kill me. I would heal easily enough if anything did happen but it would still hurt like a bitch.

I positioned myself behind Dante, straddling his precious Dragon. Where the hell were my arms supposed to go? I gasped as Dante grabbed both my arms, wrapping them around his waist. My fingers flexed as I tried to control the urge to feel every muscle under Dante's shirt.

Yup, if I ever saw this man naked I would die.

"Hold on tight." He yelled over the roaring engine.

It was the first time I was more than willing to follow his instructions. If this speed isn't fast according to Dante, I would hate to know what he defined as fast.

* * *

"Morticia it wasn't that bad. Stop being dramatic and let's go!"

I swatted away his hand, refusing his help and hopping off the bike myself. My vision went blurry and the world slipped from under my feet. I watched as Dante put his hands out to catch me from falling. It felt as though it was happening in slow motion. Dante grabbed me before my head hit the ground. He looked just as stunned as I was that he caught me, as though the world stopped for him too.

"Good reflexes." I fixed my hair as he stared at me.

"It looks perfect." He sprung one of my face-framing curls.

There goes that butterfly feeling in my southern region again.

No one has ever described my hair as perfect. It's been called many things but perfect, never. Mami always expected it to be straight for all royal events, telling me that straight hair looked more regal than a mess of curls on my head.

"Come on." Dante urged me to follow him.

I collected myself, taking a deep breath before trailing behind him.

Gods, even his ass is pure muscle.

He told me to grab a seat while he ordered for us. The bakery was painted in a baby blue color with accents of pink. There were black and white pictures all over the walls of the same man shaking hands with people who looked important. I looked around to see if I could spot the man at the shop but only a young girl with long black hair was working the cash register.

Dante gave her cash and threw some in a jar that said tips on it before rushing to me with a bottle of water.

"Drink this. I don't want you passing out on me, it's bad enough that your sugar will be spiking today." He handed me a bottle of water that was freezing cold.

Maybe I should place this water on my chest to stop this rush of heat I feel coming on from Dante being so nice to me.

"Thanks. Why are we here?"

The girl called Dante's name before he could answer me. He ran back towards me, turning his chair around before grabbing a seat.

"You need to work on your listening skills. I told you today was about research." He opened the box. My mouth watered, each baked good looking as delicious as the next.

"Excuse me for not remembering after having the traumatic experience that is you behind that beast." I pointed towards the window, where Dragon stood sparkling in the sun.

"Anyway. Today will be spent traveling to our rival bakeries to try their cookies. We need to know what we're up against, maybe adjust recipes if needed."

"Exactly how many of these sweet treats will we consume today?"

"You're complaining about eating sweets? Are you sure you didn't hit your head?" He grabbed my face, studying me.

"I love my sweets but even I have my limits."

"About twenty bakeries are competing, so cheers!" We toasted our cookies before taking a bite.

"Actually, I think I lied. There is no limit." I took another huge bite.

"It's good but not Dante good or you would've made that sound." He took another bite and raised his eyebrow.

A blush rushed to my cheeks. Thankfully Dante didn't notice because he was picking apart the cookie and examining it. Maybe I'll make it a point to do it at least once today to push his buttons. After all, it's become one of my favorite hobbies.

Chapter Thirteen

The more I rode on the back of Dragon the more comfortable I got, both with Dante's speed and with having my arms wrapped around his waist. Something about it felt like home. At every bakery, we would discover new things about each other. The conversation flowed as though we had known each other for ages. There were times when I almost slipped. Wanting to talk to him about all the amazing things that Aebriera has to offer. Dante bragged about his world travels and all I wanted to do was hit him with an: "Okay fine, but at least I've ridden a real dragon."

If only he knew he had barely scratched the surface of things to see.

"Just pick one place," Dante said while stuffing his face with another cookie.

"It's so hard to pick just one. There's too many options."

Dante moved closer to me and his hand quickly moved toward my face. He wasn't quick enough. I pinned his arm to the table.

"I wasn't going to hurt you, Morticia."

"Sorry. Reflex." I released the hold I had on his hand.

"Gun to your head, you have to choose or you're dead. GO!" He put two fingers to my temple.

"So it was an attack!"

"The clock is ticking."

"France!" I blurted out.

He disarmed himself of his fake finger 'gun' as he called it, rolling his wrist and I hoped I didn't hurt him that bad.

"Interesting. Why?"

"I read a book about it once and felt a pull towards it. The food, the culture, the museums." My eyes wandered to the black and white Eiffel Tower painting on the bakery wall.

"Well, hopefully, you don't catch any hard feelings when we crush this French bakery at the bake-off. I can't fault you though for feeling a connection to France. It took my breath away when I visited."

"Showoff," I mumbled.

"I'm sure we'll go someday." Dante took another bite of his pastry.

He said 'We'll' right? As in the two of us? I didn't just imagine a hot guy wanted to take me on a romantic vacation to Europe. Is there such a thing as sugar-induced hallucinations?

We spent a whole day together without arguing or biting each other's heads off. Dante wasn't lying about the sugar rush though, my stomach was suffering. All of the bakeries we tried were delicious, but none of them were as good as Dante's. I would never tell *him* that though. I'd rather watch him sweat. As we took our seats at our new location, Dante's body stiffened and his face hardened.

"Let's go." He grabbed my arm, pushing us through the doors.

"We just got here, Dante. What's wrong?"

"I just can't be in there right now."

"Dante if your stomach hurts just ask to use the bathroom, I'm sure it happens all the time."

"Princesa, please," he pleaded.

Did he just beg? Dante and begging are two things that don't go together. Something must be up.

I nodded my head yes and he threw my helmet at me, I barely finished strapping it on before he zoomed off.

Dante headed straight to the downstairs kitchen. He slammed pots and pans around while mumbling under his breath. I wasn't sure if I should run away from his wrath or stay put. I questioned my sanity when I decided to stay and poke at the beast standing before me.

"So are you going to throw a tantrum for the rest of the day or join me upstairs for the bottle of wine I was promised?" I crossed my arms across my chest.

Dante froze in place, slowly turning to me and glaring. His green eyes burned into me and I swore they darkened in color. My throat closed up in fear, his stare reminding me of Papi on his worst days. Days he would come home from battle in a rage because his warriors were sloppy or too many of them died. Dante didn't look like he was going to move.

I cleared my throat before I threw my bait. "If you don't join me I might just have to open all the bottles in your pretty collection."

I started to walk towards the back. My well-deserved reward awaited me and I was going to claim it. Halfway up the stairs I finally heard his footsteps behind me.

Looks like I hit the right nerve.

Dante's long strides beat me to the kitchen. His hands raked through his beard as he stared at the wall of options, pondering which wine I was worthy of. I decided to take this time to change. I've worn ball gowns, corsets, and warrior leathers but I swear to the Gods, denim will be the bane of my existence. When I emerged from the bedroom with my gray sweats on, Dante was in the same position I left him in. He hadn't moved a muscle, as if he was made of stone. A beautiful piece of art perfectly sculpted just for my enjoyment.

"Stop pretending like you're putting any actual thought into this choice. I know you're just going to open the cheapest bottle up there to give me." I rolled my eyes.

I didn't forget the part of the deal where I was to choose the bottle but he was in a crappy mood and correcting him might risk him going back on his word, resulting in zero bottles consumed. I found myself wanting to hug him. My body gravitated next to him. Fuck the wine, there was nothing I currently wanted more than to hold him. I was under the delusion that my body around his would heal whatever it was that was bothering him. I want to tell him that whatever it is, I'll help him through it just like he's helped me. That he will be okay. Dante would always be more than okay with me around and I hope he knew I could be trusted.

"Trust me, even my cheapest bottle wouldn't be cheap," Dante said without changing his stance.

"You're taking the fun out of this. Just pick one. Here." I grabbed a random bottle off of the rack.

Dante grabbed my arm and as he did a ring of fire formed in my stomach, making its way down south. He ripped the bottle out of my hand and quickly placed it back.

"Don't rush the process, please."

My mouth opened, ready to tell him to cut the shit and pick one but —

Did he just beg? Two times in one day, I can get used to this. Actually, I think I'm way too into begging Dante.

"Dante, just—" He covered my mouth with his hand and I

had to fight the urge to bite him.

"Shh Morticia. The wines are talking to me."

Once again that ring of fire formed in my lower belly.

"Okay, this one!" He pulled it off the rack releasing his grip on my mouth.

My body immediately missed his touch. I grabbed two large glasses from the cabinet.

"Wrong glasses." He swiped them from my hand and picked up a new set.

"How can it be the wrong glass? Honestly, you're lucky I even grabbed glasses, I usually chug from the bottle." I took one of the glasses from his hand to inspect it.

The glass has a long stem and a small bowl. I frowned as I thought of the amount of wine that could fit inside, barely enough to give me a buzz I bet.

"Oh I get it, you want me to drink as little as possible."

Dante followed me to the dining room, bottle and corkscrew in hand.

"I drink wine properly, the way it was intended to be consumed, not like an untrained animal. You should be put in prison for drinking straight out of the bottle. That's a criminal offense." He popped open the cork and started to pour.

"Throw me in the dungeon and throw away the key." I shrugged my shoulders as he rolled his eyes.

"This wine is a dessert wine. It's young and sweet. It's meant to be indulgent. You take your time to drink it, to enjoy it and savor its flavor." He placed the glass in front of me and swatted my hand away when I reached for it.

"Don't you think we've had enough dessert for today?"

"I can always put it back."

I rolled my eyes. "Continue."

"This is a hock wine glass. The reason that it's the perfect glass for the wine I selected is because of its shape. The shape of this glass helps our tongues, it triggers the taste buds to experience the sweetness." He swished the wine in the glass before giving it a sniff.

Dante talking about triggers in the tongue is making me hot in all the places it shouldn't be.

My whole body now felt like it was engulfed in flames. I looked at the bottle and read the label. Chateau Margaux, 1996. A wine from France.

"Okay learned my lesson now can we drink?" I grabbed my wine glass from the stem as he nodded with approval.

I took a swig of the wine and wasn't disappointed. It was delicious and had the perfect amount of sweetness.

"Wow. Pretty good stuff, Dante."

"You can taste the hints of blueberry in it. It's one of my favorites but I must admit it's not even the best one in the collection." He smirked.

"I guess I'm not good enough to taste that one huh?" I took another sip.

"I didn't say that. I've been saving it for a special occasion. Don't know what it will be or if it will happen but I want to be prepared in case it does."

I hope I'm around to see that happen.

We finished the bottle and to my surprise, he offered to open another one. I laughed when he didn't go towards the wine rack, revealing his secret stash of cheap wine from the local grocery store.

"You couldn't have told me about those?"

"You seemed like you were enjoying the beer just fine."

He laughed as I gave him a death glare and my middle finger.

"Pendejo," I said under my breath.

The wine was flowing and so were my words.

"So why wine? When did the collection start?" I asked.

"Reminds me of some important people that were in my life. I collect it to honor them in a way."

A million questions cluttered my brain. Questions that I didn't dare to ask. There was one question, however, that I needed the answer to.

"Why did we have to leave the last bakery so quickly?" I bit my lip, praying to the Gods that he wouldn't shut me out.

"We just happened to be there at the wrong time. Someone was there that I didn't want to see. Now I'm here with you and drinking cheap wine. I can't think of a better way to spend my time."

"Same." I smiled as we both raised our glasses before taking another sip.

"I haven't had a buzz like this in a while. If my Papi and Mami saw me now they would be so pissed."

"Do you still talk to your family?" Dante's eyes were soft and filled with worry as though he was scared that he crossed a line.

"I'm not able to. It's complicated, let's just say I can't be who they want me to be. I consider myself an orphan." I chugged the rest of my wine and poured another.

"That's crazy, you're perfect, and that's coming from an actual orphan."

I sat there speechless at his comment.

Perfect.

I began blushing as I saw Dante frazzled by the confession he made, he thought I was perfect. Impossible, but I was still flattered.

"I mean you're perfect in their eyes, like all parents think their kids are perfect right? Not my birth parents they're the exception to that rule since they kind of just threw me out like trash. Other than them I'm sure ninety-nine percent of parents think their children are great." He poured more red wine into our glasses, ignoring that his words were starting to slur.

"I'm so sorry for using the word orphan, I didn't mean to offend you."

"Oh don't worry you didn't. It's a part of who I am. Little orphan Dante. Annie and I should start a support group."

"Is Annie a friend of yours?" I asked as a pit of jealousy formed in my stomach.

I bet I could take her. I know I can.

"You know nothing about pop culture, do you? She's a popular comic strip that turned into a musical. She's not real so you can stand down Princesa."

"I was just curious."

"Sure you were. I didn't sense any jealousy whatsoever." Dante smirked.

I ignored his bait. "I'm sure your parents had their reasons." I grabbed the bottle from him, making the adult decision to stop for the night.

My hand made its way on top of Dante's, my thumb gently grazing his hand to comfort him. He kept his hand in mine, silently permitting me to stay connected to him.

"It's whatever. I don't even care. I'm too old to give a shit anymore and I don't need them. I had Steven and Jackie who took good care of me and loved me like I was their own. I know they truly loved me until their last breath on this earth. I have Holly and now I have you. I'm so glad I have you."

"How did they die?"

A wave of sadness flooded his face.

"You don't have to tell me if you don't want to," I whispered.

"No, it's okay, I want to."

I stayed silent, watching him take a deep breath before he spoke.

"It was date night, they made a point to have one every week. They never owned a car. It's the city you know, why would they need to? It was a nice night out so they chose to walk instead of calling a taxi when a man robbed them. The cops suspect he was a druggie who wanted a fix but had no money. He pressed his gun to my mom's back and my dad gave him everything. Everything he had on him, everything in his wallet, but as the man was about to leave sirens filled the air and spooked him. The cops got to my parents but it was too late, the man had fatally shot them both. They bled out in the street. The cops told us they were holding onto each other in their final moments, so that's sweet."

"Oh my, that's horrible, Dante." I gently squeezed his hand.

"The cops went over security footage and it was too grainy to see any of his features so they never caught the guy. That still keeps me up at night." Dante balled his hand in a fist and hit the table.

The table vibrated, causing the wine glasses to tip over.

Red wine spilled everywhere and before I could jump out of its path I was covered in it. I was unbothered about the impending stain on my clothes and more worried about the white shag rug that lay under the dining room table.

"I am so sorry! Let me get some paper towels." Dante ran to the kitchen.

A big red stain was now forming on the rug. I waved my hand over it, using my magic to make it disappear. Dante made his way back, the look of confusion was plastered on his face at the sight of the perfectly white rug.

"The wine never made it to the floor. I guess my clothes soaked it all up." I took the paper towels from his hand.

He stayed quiet and kept watching me as I patted myself dry.

"Can you stop looking at me like you killed me? It's just wine." I walked over to the trash can in the kitchen. Dante followed me as though he was my shadow.

"You missed a spot." His finger pointed to a spot on his face.

He laughed as I struggled to remove the missed spot from my face. Dante stopped me before I could make it to a mirror.

"You're hopeless. Just let me get it." He walked towards the sink to wet his thumb, before grazing the side of my bottom lip. His hand cradled my face.

"There. Perfect."

Perfect. There's that word again. If only he knew how wrong he was.

"Thank you."

His lips curved into that side smirk that I love to see. My heart raced as we stood there in silence, staring at each other, waiting for the other to move. Neither of us did.

"Did you pick a wine from France on purpose?"

"Yes." A simple answer.

"Why?" A simple question.

"Because even though you're a smart ass. You're also loving, caring, and beautiful. You deserve to experience the world outside of those books you read, Princesa. I wanted to give you a taste of what you've been missing." He tucked one of my wild curls back into place.

He smirked when it refused to stay in place and sprung free again.

I was called selfish back home. Corvina was the ungrateful

brat who wanted to explore outside of her home. The princess who would rather roam outside of the lands that have taken care of her instead of being with her people. None of that was true. I love my home. Why was it so wrong for me to want to see what else was out there? I constantly felt the guilt of wanting to explore outside the Shadow Court, yet here is Dante telling me I deserved to explore. How could he see my heart and who I was when the biggest part of me was concealed from him? Would he still feel the same if I found the courage to show him all of me? I wanted to cry but I held my tears in.

How can someone that's an admitted asshole also be one of the sweetest people I know?

I placed my hand over his and held it there, not realizing how cold I was compared to his warm touch. My gut told me to break our contact before it was too late but my body refused to move. It wanted his touch, craved it. As though Dante could read my mind, his full body pressed into mine. I could smell the wine on his breath and yearned to taste the sweetness I knew it would hold.

"Don't move." He whispered and I obeyed.

We held eye contact as he moved closer to my face. Suddenly, his lips were on mine. My heart felt like it was about to explode and I prayed to the Gods that this wasn't just another dream. He tasted as sweet as I knew he would. I felt my body go weak to his touch. In my dream, he was rough with me but right now his touch was light. His kisses were soft as though he was scared that I would recoil from him, an action I know I'm not capable of. I might be a strong fae but for him I am weak.

He pulled away and I whimpered, my body begging for more.

"We've been drinking. I don't want to take advantage of you." Dante whispered, his lips grazing mine as he spoke.

I pulled him closer to me. Leaving no space between us, already feeling his need for me as his dick poked me between my legs.

"Shut up, Pendejo!" I crashed our lips together into a kiss that left us both gasping for air.

His hands made their way to my waist. My arms were around his neck, fingers were in his hair and I couldn't help but moan as the kiss deepened. He bit my lower lip and as he did I lost all control of my body. I needed him and I needed him now. I broke our kiss to take off his shirt, gasping in awe as I saw how hot he looked shirtless, finally getting to see all of the muscles I felt all day. My lips found their way to his tattoos.

"You really do love dragons don't you?" I asked as I admired the scaly black dragon wrapped around his right bicep.

"In school, kids used to make fun of me when they asked what my favorite animal was and I replied with dragons. They would say 'dragons aren't real dumb ass' so I made sure to have a real dragon by my side forever."

Oh, how I wish I could prove all those kids wrong.

I smiled, kissing every inch of his tattoo as I made my way down to take off his pants. Before I could he grabbed my face, forcing me back up to him for another breathtaking kiss.

If this is how I die then so be it, I'll thank the Gods that it was a mercifully beautiful death.

Dante pulled down my stained pants, revealing the black lace underneath.

"Fuck." He growled before claiming my lips again.

He lifted me as if I weighed nothing, placing me on the kitchen counter without breaking the kiss that was turning from sweet to savage. My head started to pound, distracting me from this glorious moment with this beautiful man.

Did I hit my head?

With every kiss, the pounding became more intense. I clawed at my shirt, my breasts begging to be released from the bra I was wearing. Dante took the hint and freed me.

Dante licked his lips, "You're fucking beautiful."

"I bet I'll look gorgeous once you're inside me." I tugged down his pants, my hand going inside the waistband of his underwear.

My Gods, he was as ready for me as I was for him. The pain continued and so did my annoyance. I wanted to give Dante all of my attention because he deserves it but the pounding in my head was becoming too much of a distraction. Dante's lips made their way down my neck as his hand grabbed one of my breasts.

"Trust me, every inch of me will be inside of you soon enough. Be patient, Princesa. I want to take my time with you."

Fuck I needed this. I needed him more than I needed air, more than anything I thought I ever needed in my life and if I didn't have him this second my body felt like it would combust.

He bit down on my neck as his fingers trailed their way down my stomach, stopping right where I wanted them. As his fingers moved in slow circles, my back arched off the back of the kitchen cabinet. Finally, the pounding in my head stopped.

"Dante," I whispered in pleasure.

The relief was short-lived. The pleasure was replaced with unbearable pain. It was as if a floodgate opened in my brain and filled with images. Screaming started to fill the room as the images flashed before me. I didn't realize they were my screams until Dante jumped back, almost knocking over the wine racks on the other side of the wall. My screams of pain only got louder and the vision kept coming to me. The visions are blurry but remind me of my dreams, jumping around to different images.

Papi's crown, sitting on the armrest of his throne.

Mami sobbed over Papi's body. A dagger sticking out of his chest.

Mami was engulfed in dark magic.

Lastly, a white light bursts through the battlefield and fae warriors get slaughtered.

Dante was shaking me, trying to get me out of this trance. Both of his hands cradled my face.

"Corvina, please! Morticia, please! Are you okay? You're freaking me out!" He screamed.

The visions stopped and my eyes couldn't stop blinking. I wanted to make sure that what I was seeing was real. Dante was in front of me horrified and I was unsure if he was scared *for* me or *of* me. He backed away slowly as I jumped down from the kitchen counter.

"Your eyes. There were pictures in your eyes." he shuddered as he spoke and kept staring at me.

"You're just drunk. It was one of those headaches again but I'm fine." I grabbed the blanket off the couch to cover myself as I walked towards the front door.

"I'll see you tomorrow." I opened the front door but he didn't budge.

I needed time to myself to try to understand what the fuck just happened to me.

"I know what I saw! Don't gaslight me." His voice was shaky.

Dante is staring at me looking for an explanation, an explanation that I couldn't give. There was nothing that I could say that would make sense to him. Even if I did tell him the truth of what just happened, would he believe me? Or would he think he just tried to have sex with a crazy woman who believed she was fae from a different realm? I tried to rack my brain for a believable explanation but I knew no explanation would do. My heart slowly breaks as I realize what must be done. I'm growing tired of making decisions that hurt me and others around me.

He flinched as I made my way to him and it felt like a sword to the chest. "I'll tell you everything. Please don't be afraid of me."

"I could never be afraid of you."

I smiled somberly as I intertwined our fingers and before he could question me any further, I kissed him.

My magic worked its way through my body and into his. The kiss that will undo everything about this night. Dante will forget what could've been. Our kiss deepened, replacing his memory of tonight with a new one. As far as he's concerned our kiss never happened. We drank, had a couple of laughs and he slept on the couch because he was too drunk to get back home.

A tear rolled down my cheek as I pulled back from the kiss, watching him move to the couch and fall asleep. He'll wake up oblivious to the truth of what happened today. I just wiped away a memory that I want to relive forever. A memory that will haunt me for the rest of my days as my body will now forever ache for his touch.

The next morning Dante snuck out of the apartment without saying goodbye. It wasn't until I knew he was gone that I allowed myself to pour my heart out, finally releasing all the tears I wanted to last night.

I shot Holly a text, letting her know that I couldn't make it to work today. There was no way I could concentrate on anything else today other than getting the answers I needed. Last night was the first time I've ever seen visions and it's too much of a coincidence that they mirror the nightmares I've been having.

As much as I don't want to, I open a portal back home.

"Gods, if you can hear me please help. I need the Oracle."

Chapter Fourteen

My chest feels heavy as I stand in the middle of the field, breathing in the air of a place that is so familiar to me. I forgot how nice it feels not to be an outsider, to be around people and places you know. These fields are only used during the Golden Blossom Festival of lights.

When the golden blossoms are in full bloom they shoot out rays of light into the sky, an unforgettable view. Every corner of this field holds a memory close to my heart. My first time at the festival with Mami and Papi. Having my first kiss under one of the trees, the poor guy ran away as he saw my papi approaching us and I cried as he threatened to kill anybody that dared touch me. Having a picnic with the only person brave enough to be my friend and ruining our friendship when I realized I wanted to be more than just a friend. Meeting my first love, the same love that gifted me my first heartbreak. It's crazy how a place that has brought me so much joy can also bring me so much sadness.

"Child, do you know there is a bounty on your head?" The Oracle greeted me.

Golden blossom fields are where Oracles like to gather. No one comes here when they aren't in full bloom. There aren't many Oracles that still roam Aebriera, a lot of them are hunted.

I've grown fond of this Oracle, she was sweet to me, unlike all the others I tried to speak to. Oracles I've tracked down in the past have refused to talk to me because of who my parents are or because they know I am their blind spot. This Oracle is a friend, a confidant, and an amazing listener. She never got frustrated with me and agreed to work with me to find a way for Oracles to see me.

"Done with the human world so soon?" She asked.

I jumped into her arms, apologizing as soon as I felt her wince. She's so much more fragile than the last time I saw her. Oracles age faster than most creatures due to their power. There are streaks of white hair in place of where her black hair used to be. She's wearing an emerald green cloak covered in gold embroidered vines. Her pale white hands were covered in age spots and her nails were painted a blood red. She adjusted her cloak and as she looked at me I couldn't help notice that her gray eyes were sunken in and she looked so tired. I couldn't handle seeing visions for one night, it's unimaginable what kind of toll it can have on you if it was a daily occurrence.

"If I knew there was a bounty on my head I would've found another way to get my answers. I've recently discovered a cell phone, an amazing invention. I wonder if it would work in this world?"

"A lot has happened since you decided to leave, Corvina. Yes, there is a bounty on your head and it's a hefty one so don't tempt me to turn you in." She knelt to smell a golden blossom that had started to bloom.

"You would never. You have a soft spot for me to go along with that blind spot."

"Actually, there's just a soft spot. The blind spot is no longer there."

"Excuse me?"

"I say there is a bounty on your head and you scream to attract attention? Calm down child before you get us both killed." She rolled her eyes as she grabbed my arm.

I followed her lead as she moved us behind a nearby tree.

"I'm sorry but you can understand my shock. Is it just you? What worked? What made you see me? When did you start to see me? I'm asking too many questions, aren't I? I'm sorry, continue." I covered my mouth with my hand, having to physically stop myself from talking.

"The day you left for the human realm I felt it. I have no explanation as to why, some of our oldest Oracles are still trying to find an answer. It was as though something clicked. As soon as you went through that portal I received a vision and so did the others. It was like a door unlocked and flooded us with all your possible futures. I saw you coming today wanting to speak to me but you came with a man and now I see you are alone. Very odd." She crossed her legs as she sat down on a tree stump.

"Did you send me those visions that I had last night?"

"You're having visions? Faes don't have visions. If they did there would be no need for my breed's existence. Sending visions is beyond our abilities."

"I know we can't. Yet, here I am looking for answers because I had visions! You're my friend and I trust you. There's a cloaking spell on me so if there is someone out there with a power like this they must be powerful." My nerves started getting the best of me as I paced back and forth.

"It's possible, but a power of that magnitude has not been seen in centuries. You know as well as I do that if anyone dared to show that amount of power off your father would have their head. May the Gods rest his soul." Her hands went to her chest as she lowered her head.

My heart stopped and the world went still.

"Gods rest his soul?" my throat went dry.

"Yes, the king is dead and in his place has risen something far worse. Our people were lied to, told his death was a peaceful one from the one disease in the world that can claim a faes life. The announcement from the palace told your people that his death was without malice but this is not true. He was stabbed in the chest by your mother. Only the Oracles know the truth, but none will speak the truth in fear of their life." Her eyes filled with dread upset that she had to be the one to tell me this news.

My first vision.

"That doesn't make sense, why would she do such a thing? She loves him!" I felt a pain in my chest.

"Just because you love someone doesn't mean you're not willing to betray them. You're still young and will learn this lesson soon enough." Her hand rested on my shoulder, trying to give me comfort that never came.

"I know my Mami. She would not do this of her own accord. She would've burned the world for him." None of this made sense. I refuse to believe it.

"Hold my hand, I will show you what I have seen. My eyes do not lie." She held out her hand's palms up.

I grabbed a hold of her hands. What the Oracle said was true. She showed me as they argued ferociously and Mami grabbed Papi's dagger. She stabbed him in the middle of his chest and I felt the tears forming in my eyes as I watched his body fall to the floor. Then there it was, the vision that I saw in the kitchen last night of her sobbing on the floor over his body. The Oracle took back her hands and the vision ended.

"No. You said that your vision of today was wrong. What's to say that this is true?" I grabbed her hands and put them back into mine, intertwining them so she couldn't let go.

"You've never questioned my abilities before. I know it is a hard truth to swallow."

"I have to see more, I need to find out why! There has to be a reason why!" The tears that were forming were now a waterfall on my face.

"Corvina, that is all there is to see. The Gods gifted me with that vision and nothing else. This I swear to you." She tried to loosen my grip but my power was too strong.

"Do not lie to me!" I kept squeezing her hands, my nails digging into her skin.

My body was frigged and I felt a vibration go through me. The sky was turning cloudy and purple smoke started to surround us. It felt like my body wanted to explode, as though all the power I'd held back since being in the human realm wanted to burst out. There was a voice inside my head telling me to end her, that she was lying to me and she must be punished. My breath was quickening and I could feel my nails digging deeper and deeper into her skin. If she wouldn't show me willingly I would take her visions by force, I would find a way to see what I want to see.

"I would not benefit from lying. Never have I lied to you and I would not start now. Please, let go." Her voice trembled in fear.

I looked down at her hands and they were covered in blood. The sight of it snapped me out of my trance. This was an unfamiliar feeling that I never want to experience again. I couldn't recognize myself as I stared at my reflection in her eyes. My hands quickly released hers and I continued to sob, dropping to my knees.

"I'm sorry for your hands. May I?" I gesture to her hands. She met me on the ground, hesitantly agreeing to my request.

Using my power, I fixed her bloody hands, making them look as though nothing had happened. Hurting my friend is the last thing I ever want to do but at least I have the power to fix it.

"Your people are grieving. Not only for the loss of your father but also for the loss of their true queen, you. They will not know true grief until they are under the reign of your mother. She is already preparing to take over and your mother will destroy us all. Her coronation is set to happen in a week's time. Carmela is a powerful fae but somehow with your father's passing it's as though her power has grown. I can sense a power shift."

Everything went according to my plan. The weight of the crown is no longer on my head. I should be elated yet I'm horrified. To think that her taking over would mean my people would suffer at her hand felt like a dagger to my heart. None of this makes sense and my head is in a fog. I came here for answers and I'm leaving with more questions.

"What you showed me, it's part of the visions I was shown yesterday. I saw four visions. Mami sobbed over Papi's body and his body had a dagger in his chest, just like the one you just showed me. Papi's crown was sitting on his throne and Mami picked it up and placed it on her head. Mami was enveloped in dark magic. The last vision is one I've seen multiple times in my dreams. There is white light bursting through the battlefield and fae warriors getting slaughtered."

"Corvina. All of those visions are ones I've also had. They've all haunted me, all except for the last one. That's our salvation."

Chapter Fifteen

It's been days since my visit home and I still haven't recovered. It had slapped me in the face with some hard truths. The entity that haunts my dreams is the same thing that will save my people. How do I find it and how am I supposed to know exactly what I'm looking for? The meeting with the Oracle was brief. I couldn't risk being there longer than needed and she couldn't help me find the mysterious being.

"It's your journey that you must embark on on your own. To interfere in it would be to laugh at the Gods."

Dramatic much?

I left my home with a heavy heart and confusion swimming in my brain. I wanted to ask her about Dante if she was able to see humans as she sees us but I stopped myself. His name shouldn't be spoken there. I need him and Holly to be safe.

My body wanted to collapse the minute I went back through the portal. The sleepless nights were getting to me and Holly's offer of something she called melatonin sounded Gods sent. All the questions started to jumble in my head; feeling like an impossible puzzle that only talking to Mami directly would solve. It's a risk I'm not willing to take. If she was willing to take Papi's life as the Oracle said, what's to stop her from taking my friends from me, the life I've built for myself here? Dante and Holly have made my life in the human world enjoyable.

Holly and I had our weekly shopping trips and lunches which I grew to love. Dante and I have kept our bickering to a maximum of only twice a week. Working at the shop stopped feeling like work and I was able to save up quite enough money. I tried to start paying Dante for occupying the apartment, but that caused a fight. If he won't accept my money I'll have to force a gift onto him. What could I possibly gift someone that would equal my gratitude for him giving me a home? It's times like these that I wish they knew all the parts of me, because a gift that I could get them from back home would beat anything I can get them here in this realm, plus it wouldn't hurt to have unlimited funds at my disposal.

I let the bed swallow me whole. It was the first decent sleep I've had since arriving here. I heard a light knock on the front door followed by the door swinging open.

"Ugh," I groaned, refusing to move a muscle.

There are only two people it could be and Holly doesn't have a key. You would think the man can take a hint. The bedroom door is clearly closed for a reason.

"Are you decent?" he asked through the crack of the bedroom door.

"Actually, no. I'm completely naked. The sheets are now tainted with my bare flesh." I said hoping he would get the hint to leave me be.

"Was that an invitation? I'm flattered, but I don't mix business with pleasure."

Little do you know.

He opened the bedroom door letting himself in, pretending to be disappointed when he saw me fully clothed.

"What if I was naked in here."

"Well, then I would've gone blind and had to burn the sheets."

We almost rolled around in these sheets, but sure. Hide how you really feel.

I chucked my pillow at his head and unlike the cookie, he was ready for it.

"You have to stop throwing things at me. It's becoming predictable."

This was the first time I'd seen him since our wine night. I've been avoiding him at all costs, coming up with reasons why he couldn't see me. I told him I was sick and as I looked at him now, I felt sick to my stomach. I hated lying to him more than I already was. Not only was I starting to feel physically ill, but my throat felt dry as Dante stared at me. His hair was under a baseball cap which he decided to wear backwards.

Holy shit, why is this hot? Why am I turned on by this man wearing a baseball cap the wrong way?

I couldn't help but stare back. His eyes were shining bright as the daylight entered through the bedroom blinds.

Focus Corvina!

"May I ask why you're here at this ungodly hour?"

"It's 10:00 am." He folded his arms across his chest, completely unamused.

"My question still stands."

"I just wanted to see how you were feeling."

Now I actually might throw up from the guilt. The concerned look on his face is killing me.

Why did this Pendejo have to be caring right now when I'm trying to distance myself.

"I also made you some soup. I left it on the kitchen counter, it's chicken noodle." He placed his hands in his jeans pockets as he leaned against the bedroom wall.

Mierda.

"Thank you. I'm feeling much better."

"Yeah, no problem." He started to walk towards the bedroom door to leave.

He paused as he started to close the door behind him. "I wanted to know if you were feeling better to see if you wanted to join me. I wanted to reward you for all your hard work training for the bake-off."

This is a bad idea. Horrible idea. I shouldn't entertain the idea at all. Be strong Corvina.

"I was planning to stay in and read all day." A lie.

"If you insist. You're missing out though. It's going to be *really* fun."

Well damn, he's officially piqued my interest. I know I shouldn't be this excited to spend one-on-one time that didn't involve baking with Dante but my heart can't help but flutter at the thought. Every cell in my body is telling me I should ignore him, but that stupid bitch I call my heart is determined to get me in trouble.

"Wait!" I jumped up from the bed to stop him from leaving the apartment.

I ran and caught him right as his hand gripped the front door handle. I grabbed his forearm. "Define *really* fun."

"It's a surprise, Morticia." His grin came attached with a sparkle in his eye that I didn't trust.

"Is this going to be another Dragon situation? I am not riding any more dangerous things, Dante. I am good for the next millennia." I arched my brow as I studied his face.

"Can you just trust me? I even rented a car for us." He held out a pair of keys, jiggling them as his mischievous grin grew.

Dante brushed his hand over my arm and his touch caused instant goosebumps on my skin.

"Fine."

I started to walk over to the bedroom when the aroma hit me. The soup Dante had cooked for me sat on the counter.

One little taste before we go wouldn't hurt.

The spoon touched my lips and as I slowly slurped up the soup my eyes rolled to the back of my head.

Dammit, that's good soup. Can this man make anything that isn't delicious?

I closed the bedroom door behind me, getting ready for whatever adventure Dante had planned for us.

"It was the best soup you've ever had wasn't it," Dante questioned me from the other side of the door.

"Shut up. It was fine." I heard Dante chuckle.

"So what did you name this one?" I asked Dante as I threw on a graphic tee.

"The car? I can't name her or I'll get too attached," he said.

I emerged from the bedroom with a smug smile on my face "Her? Sorry to break it to you, it sounds like you're already attached."

"Well, I'm not going to say he, I have to be inside the damn thing."

"So you're straight. Noted. Machismo ass."

"That's a new one."

"You know what isn't? Pendejo. Now where was it you said we were going again?"

Dante threw a pillow at my head, which I gracefully dodged.

"Nice try. Hurry up, we have places to be."

I threw on a jean jacket. "I'm going to plead with you just like I did with Dragon. *Please* bring me back home in one piece."

"Cross my heart and hope you don't die," he said.
Dante winked and my heart skipped a beat.

Chapter Sixteen

Dante opened the car door for me and as I slid into my seat I couldn't help checking him out as he walked over to the driver's side.

Can this man ever look unattractive?

I'd never been in a car before and it was a disappointment to find out there was no need to hold onto Dante during the joyride.

"For someone so worried about dying you should put on your seat belt." Dante turned on the car and I jumped as the music started playing.

It's astonishing how music can be played through an invention they created called speakers and radios. I was amazed when I first heard about them during training. I pressed a little red button and music soared throughout the store. Holly even taught me how to get music to play from my phone. The music here is very different from what we have back home but I honestly enjoy it.

"Do not judge me when I tell you this- I've never been in a car before," I said without making eye contact with him.

"What did you use for transportation back home?"

Portals. Dragons. Pegasuses.

"Anything but a car."

I would love to have a day where I don't embarrass myself around him. Is that too much to ask? While I'm asking the Gods for things, can they also stop me from getting heart palpitations whenever he looks at me?

Dante reached over me and my body went still. His face was inches from mine and if I dared move our lips would touch. His eyes stayed glued to mine as he brought around a piece of polyester fabric with a metal buckle on the end. The buckle snapped into another piece that was by my left hip. He winked at me as he pulled away. Cool, confirmation that the Gods are in fact ignoring me because I swear my heart just leaped out of my chest.

"Ah, the infamous seat belt I presume." I pulled on the strap that was now lying across my chest.

"You know I'm still trying to figure out what planet you're from and if you come in peace." His fingers made a weird gesture that I didn't understand.

I chuckled nervously.

"*Star Trek?*" He was pointing to his hand.

When I didn't respond he just shook his head, his face a mixture of disappointment and disapproval.

"We're going to have a day to watch both *Star Wars* and *Star Trek*. Holly is going to be a little too happy about that." He rolled his eyes at the thought of her excitement.

"Can you please make this contraption move so we can get to wherever we're going?"

"So snippy today. You're about to have the time of your life!" His hand moved to a stick that had PRNDL printed onto the side of it.

"I'm sorry. I haven't been sleeping well, I have a lot on my mind."

I turned towards my window, watching all of the buildings zoom by. I could feel Dante's eyes staring at me, my body felt as if it was burning.

I changed the subject in hopes he would let it go. "Nothing that you have to worry about. It won't interfere with your precious bake-off."

He stayed silent. If he didn't say anything soon I would go insane.

"Why aren't we getting some last-minute baking in? Pretty confident in us huh?"

"Way to deflect. If you don't want to talk about it, that's fine. But for someone who hates silence, I'm shocked you wouldn't want to." He shrugged his shoulders.

"I do perfectly fine in silence." The second lie I told him today.

"Sure." Dante narrowed his eyes.

I remained quiet to prove my point. My leg began to shake.

"The minute it's quiet you look like you want to crawl out of your skin."

By the look on Dante's face, I was miserably failing at proving that point. "Are you done analyzing me or?" I asked.

He chuckled before zooming onto the busy road. The majority of the car ride was spent asking Dante where we were going and he constantly refused to tell me. When I finally decided to give up he raised the radio's volume. Though no words were being exchanged it felt good to be in his company, as though my mind could finally relax and stop overthinking. My eyes started to feel heavy and my breathing became shallow. It wouldn't hurt to rest my eyes for five minutes.

"Princesa, it's time to wake up from your slumber. Such a passenger princess for someone who was scared for her life with me behind the wheel," Dante whispered.

As I jolted awake, my left hand found its way around his throat. Dante's hands were in the air as he strained his voice to speak.

"It's me, it's Dante."

I gasped and released my hold on him.

"I am so sorry, Dante."

"It's okay, next time warn me when you want to live out one of your kinky fantasies. Is that what you were dreaming about?" Dante wiggled his eyebrows at me and I wanted to die from the humiliation.

"I was going to check you for a pulse but then I heard you snoring so I knew you were alive."

There goes more of that humiliation.

"I do not snore! Now you're just making shit up. Where are we anyway?"

I looked out of the window to find that we were surrounded by other cars on a patch of grass, from a distance I could see a big wheel of some sort that looked like it was moving in slow motion.

"You don't snore in your sleep just like you don't drool." He pointed at my chin and as he handed me a napkin.

I wiped at my chin and felt my face get hot as I saw the drool on the napkin.

Can one die from too much humiliation?

"It's a fair! Before you ask what a fair is, get out of the car and I can just show you." Dante rolled his eyes.

Dante made his way over to my side of the car to open the door. The seat belt stopped me as I tried to get out, pulling me back into my seat hard. Dante looked like he was about to burst from trying to control his laughter. I gave him a deadly glare as he tried to compose himself. He reached over me and pressed a red button that released the seat belt. Not only did Dante look amazing, but he also smelled like a dream. A mixture of cedar wood and blood orange invaded my nose.

Did he spray something on himself while I was asleep or did I just never notice how amazing he smelled before today?

To be fair we were always baking so maybe the sweets masked his wonderful scent but now that I've gotten a taste of it it's the only scent I ever want to smell.

We made our way towards that big wheel in the sky. People were everywhere and I couldn't help but smile at the sound of children's laughter. Dante had me wait for him as he went in line to purchase something. Along with the big wheel that I saw from the car there are multiple little contraptions the humans are indulging in. If I didn't see them smiling with my own eyes I would think they were getting into torturing devices. Dante came back with a bunch of colored papers in his hand.

"I got us a bunch of tickets to ride the rides and play games." He handed me a handful to hold onto.

"You want me to get on that?" I pointed to the big wheel with fear in my eyes.

"We don't have to start on the Ferris wheel. There are other rides we ride in the meantime and work our way up you scaredy cat. Plus I want to kick your ass at some carnival games. If I win a stuffed animal do not think I'm winning it for you. That bad boy will be all mine." He pointed at a giant stuffed unicorn that had a rainbow-colored tail.

That is not an accurate depiction of a unicorn at all.

Dante grabbed my hand, his fingers intertwined with mine, dragging me onto our first ride. His hand in mind fits so perfectly it's terrifying. He handed the tickets to a woman before we hopped onto one of the horses. I couldn't help but notice the number of children on the ride with their parents. It dawned on me that this ride was made specifically for children.

"You have little faith in me don't you." I snarled at Dante.

He sat down on a white horse next to me.

"We have to get the boring ones out of the way or would you rather start with the Hyper-loop?" He pointed at a ride, the sight of it made my stomach drop.

"No, but still. Let's get off. We look ridiculous." I was doing my best to ignore the strangers who were staring at us.

"I don't know about you but I look quite dashing. Like a prince on his great white steed." He puffed out his chest and I couldn't help but laugh.

"Besides, why care about what other people think? As long as you're happy that's what matters. Are you happy, Morticia?"

"Eh. Could be happier."

"You'll be filled with joy once this thing starts moving. Te lo prometo, " he said with a smirk.

"Pendejo, are you learning Spanish?" I asked, my mouth agape.

Dante didn't have the chance to answer as the ride started. I held onto the pole of my horse tightly as it moved. My grip slowly loosened as I realized how slow it was going.

Dammit, he was right and made good on his promise. I am getting a little bit filled with joy.

As I look at the horses, I can't help but think about when Papi built a whole ranch for Mami as a gift for their anniversary. She's from a small village, and her parents were farmers. When her parents' farm wasn't producing enough money to support the family, she enlisted in the army to become a warrior, as it paid well. If it weren't for my Mami becoming the warrior that she is, she never would've met Papi. Seeing all of these families here is beautiful, but it also reminds me of how my family is destroyed because of me. The horses came to a halt, and I jolted off my seat. I'm tired of playing it safe, of running away from things that scare me.

"Let's go to the Hyper-loop!"

"Are you sure?"

"What? Are you scared? I taunted him.

A wicked smile took over Dante's face. "Race you there."

Chapter Seventeen

I've concluded that I love the fair! Did I throw up the funnel cake that Dante bought for me? Absolutely! Do I regret riding the Star-ship 3000? Hell no! This has been the most fun I've had in a while. I hate to admit it but Dante was right.

"I told you I was going to kick your ass." Dante gloated as we walked away from the game booth.

"Congratulations, you are now the proud owner of a plush unicorn. You won because that game is rigged. How is anyone supposed to toss a ring around those bottles?" I rolled my eyes as he wiggled the monstrosity in my face.

I noticed a little girl in the corner, eyeing that stupid-looking unicorn that Dante was holding with sparkles in her eyes.

"You know you're jealous." He kissed the top of its head.

"I'm not at the slightest, but your new pet has a secret admirer." I nudged my head towards the little girl's direction.

Dante started walking towards her.

He isn't about to do what I think he is about to do.

The little girl's pigtails bounced up and down as she strangled the unicorn Dante handed to her.

"Jealous now?" he questioned me.

No, but I think my heart is about to combust.

I grabbed the cap off his head, putting it on my own. "Nope."

"I can't even pretend to be mad when it looks good on you."

Was that an actual compliment?

"Thanks. Even though I have no clue what the symbol on it means."

His black hat was embroidered with the letters 'NY' in a stylized script. The script is orange with a blue outline.

"Please don't tell me you're a *Yankees* fan or I'm going to have to rip my *Mets* hat off of that pretty big head of yours."

"I don't have a big head. It's normal sized, I just have a lot of hair!"

"So am I ripping the hat off your 'normal sized head' or?"

"I'm not going to lie to you, Dante. I didn't understand a word that just came out of that pretty mouth of yours."

"So you think my mouth is pretty?" he smirked.

I rolled my eyes, "I think we should get something sweet." I grabbed Dante's hand trying to drag him towards a sweets stand.

"You haven't had enough to eat yet? Or are you delaying the inevitable that is us riding the Ferris wheel." He furrowed his brows.

"I'm sorry, are you calling me fat?" A look of horror took over my face as I pretended to be offended by his statement.

I've done what I thought was impossible. Dante is completely flustered.

"No. I would never. Your curves are perfect. I didn't mean..." He stopped stumbling over his words when he saw my grin of amusement.

"You're an ass." He lightly punched my arm.

"If you recall I threw up my funnel cake so I need to replace it with another sweet. It's written in the scrolls."

"Scrolls? Oh, so you're not an alien you're a time traveler. Where is your Delorean?"

"My what?"

"Jesus, we're adding *Back to the Future* to the movie watch list. Anyway, where can I read this scroll?" Dante crossed his arms around his chest.

"It's right next to that stupid paper of rules you had taped to the fridge door." I rolled my eyes.

"You never read that, did you? Too busy reading your filthy books?" He wiggled his eyebrows at me.

It was my turn to punch his arm, and I didn't hold back. I couldn't hold back my look of satisfaction as he winced and rubbed his bicep. After I crumpled up his stupid list and threw it at Dante's head it mysteriously ended up on the bedroom dresser. I just flipped it over and haven't looked at it since. Though I gave no thought to his stupid list since that day, I have had many thoughts about those *Fifty Shades* books. I devoured the whole series. We each got an ice cream cone as big as the head of that ridiculous unicorn Dante won.

"Okay I approve of this detour, this ice cream is fucking delicious." Dante licked his cone.

The way he licked his ice cream should be illegal and the fact he's giving me direct eye contact as he does is making my knees buckle. My mind flashed back to how good his tongue felt wrestling with mine, how amazing he tasted. I broke eye contact before I did something I would regret.

"Whelp here goes nothing," I said as I stared down the Ferris wheel, cringing at the rust.

"I promise it's as safe as anything else you rode today. Do you trust me?" Dante held out his hand.

"Never." I grabbed his hand.

My heart was pounding and my hands were sweating pro-fusely. He guided me inside our pod and even though my hands felt like a swamp, Dante didn't let go. I would be a fool to think of this as anything but a kind gesture but even so, my heart still fluttered from the contact.

As the wheel rotated and we rose higher into the sky I couldn't help but marvel at the view. "Wow."

"The city is beautiful at night, isn't it? There's nothing like seeing it from here." Dante let go of my hand, sensing my calm.

If I didn't know what real magic was I would dare to say it's magical. I jumped as a loud booming noise filled the air. I looked to the right of me and a huge metal contraption flew through the sky, high in the clouds.

"I take it you've never been on an airplane before. I don't blame you for being freaked out by one, it's definitely not my favorite form of transportation." He shook off the chills I saw forming on his arm.

"Wait, you're scared of something? Never thought I'd see the day." I put my hand to my chest and gasped.

"I'm honored that you believe me to be so courageous that I would have zero fears but that's far from the truth." He smirked.

"Oh yeah, why don't you enlighten me? Other than flying, what is the great Dante... I just realized that I don't know your last name."

"It's Cole."

Our pod was now at the very top of the Ferris wheel and came to a complete stop. Dante had warned me before going on that this would happen so I wouldn't freak out.

"Okay then Mr. Cole, what are you afraid of? "

"Being a disappointment. Holly is so much like my parents

and I'm just not. I'm terrified that they regretted adopting me. That they died ashamed of me." His eyes were locked on the city below us.

The mere thought that he could disappoint anyone is ludicrous. He might be a pain in the ass but he's amazing.

"I understand that. I could never be what my parents wanted me to be. The fact that I'm so different from them… I wish I could change who I am, and be a version of myself that I know they want me to be. They would never directly tell me to change but I know the truth. I can't live a lie." His eyes met mine, his gaze was soft.

I hadn't noticed that Dante's hand had made its way to my thigh, trying to console me with his touch. My mouth started to tremble and I could feel the tears collecting in my eyes. I went to turn my head away from him, not wanting Dante to see me wiping away my tears. Being an emotional wreck was another trait I've desperately tried to change. His hand moved from my thigh, holding my chin between his thumb and index finger to try and keep me in place. He forced me to face him, keeping his grip on my chin. His thumb on his right hand wiped away the tear that had escaped. My throat felt so dry that it was hard to swallow as Dante and I stared at each other silently. His hand moved from my chin to cup my face, his fingers tangled in my hair. Dante's green eyes glowed, shining brightly from the fair lights. He licked his bottom lip as his face inched closer to me. His lips brushed mine and suddenly we were both jolted in our seats as the Ferris wheel started to move again. We both scrambled to separate ourselves. I cleared my throat and it was completely silent as we made our way to the ground. As soon as it was our turn to disembark I sprinted as fast as I could.

"I'm going to use the bathroom before we head out," I moved, unclear if I was even going in the right direction.

Where the hell is the bathroom again?

If I just listened to my brain earlier today this situation could have been avoided. I wouldn't be put in this predicament.

Corvina, qué estás haciendo? Hay que pensar con la cabeza ,no con el corazón.

The memory of our first kiss is now all I can think about and it's hurting me more now than it already did. I blamed the wine for that night that we kissed but no wine touched our lips tonight. Was it out of pity? Did he want the girl who felt unworthy of her family to feel wanted? The thought made me feel sick or maybe it's all the fried food I ate.

Yup, I need a bathroom. Now.

After I threw up, I felt the hairs on the back of my neck stand up as I exited the restroom. Someone was watching me, I could feel their eyes burning into me. I continued walking back to Dante when someone popped out at me. My reflexes kicked in and I used the palm of my hand to attack, striking them with my palm in an upward forward motion right to their nose. They yelped, covering their face. I was getting ready to attack again, reaching for my blade, when they put their hands up to surrender.

"Holy shit Corvina. Your Mami taught you well, she would be proud of that defensive work." My body went numb with the sound of his voice.

I stood in shock. I haven't heard him say my name in so long. My heart dropped to my stomach as I looked at him with disbelief. The last time I saw him we were in the golden blossom field, my heart breaking into a million pieces.

"Elias," I whispered.

He smirked. "Hola, mi cariño."

Chapter Eighteen

I've read books about panic attacks and I always thought that people were exaggerating the symptoms but right now I feel like I'm going to die. My chest is tight, I can barely breathe and the whole world is spinning.

"Whoa, Corvina breathe." Elias' hand made its way to my back.

Ironic isn't it? That the person causing me stress is trying to help take it away. I would laugh if I wasn't so focused on my breathing. What does it say about me that it's working?

"I need a minute." I walked over to a nearby bench to sit down, staring at the floor trying to steady my breath.

Elias Murano sat next to me and his hand found its way from my back down to my thighs. I had forgotten how calming his presence could be. How quickly my body accepts his touch.

This would be my luck, what are the chances that my ex-fiancé is here? The Gods really must love playing games with me. Elias, the son of Clemente Murano, my Papi's right-hand man. Clemente means merciful but that man is anything but, which made him the perfect choice to head the Royal Guard. Elias was always around growing up and I didn't blame him. His home life was one that I wouldn't want even for my worst enemy. His older brother is the center of attention, therefore he is always trying to compete with him for his father's affection. His twin sister is the worst. She and I never got along, she can never do wrong in his parent's eyes. She's only three minutes younger than Elias, yet her mother treats her like she's still in diapers. Elias' mother, Amora, was blessed by the Gods looks-wise but she's not the brightest, making her easy prey for the cruelty of having Clemente Murano as your husband.

My gaze moved from the floor to his eyes. I never found dark brown eyes beautiful until I met him, but to be fair everything about Elias is beautiful. His face is always freshly shaven, jaw sharp enough to cut diamonds. His jet-black hair was perfectly shaved on the sides, and the curls on his head had zero frizz. It's been months since I've seen him but every muscle on his body has stayed perfectly molded, some looking even bigger than before. Our breakup was anything but cordial and every emotion I had that day threatened to come spilling out.

A familiar voice broke my focus. "Is there a problem here?"

I looked up and there Dante was, standing in front of us. His face was hard as stone as he stared down Elias. Dante's eyes moved over to Elias' hand on my thigh and his jaw clenched. I moved my thigh quickly, making his hand fall. As I watched Dante, guilt washed over me. Why do I feel like I'm betraying Dante by being so close to Elias? Maybe it's because we were about to kiss and now I am intimately close to another man. A man he doesn't know I had a history with.

This doesn't look good at all.

"She's perfectly fine, I've got her." Elias stood up, making his way towards Dante.

One of the reasons I fell for Elias, other than how devastatingly handsome he is, was how protective he was of me. That trait, however, is not working in my favor at the moment.

Elias is intimidating; anyone with common sense would avoid conflict with him, but Dante doesn't flinch. My body wants to move off the bench but part of me wants to see these two titans go at it, so I stay seated.

"No offense dude but I wasn't talking to you." Dante walked past Elias, bumping into his shoulder on his way to sit next to me. Elias' hands balled into a fist.

Dante whispered, "Do you know this creep or do I have to kick his ass?"

Hot. Why is this scenario so hot? Snap out of it Corvina this is real life, not one of your romance novels.

"Yeah, unfortunately, I know him." I placed myself between them to create a barrier. *No one will be kicking anyone's ass, no matter how hot and bothered the idea of it is currently making me.*

"Elias, this is Dante. Dante, this is Elias."

Dante put his left hand on my lower back and extended his right hand out to Elias.

"Nice to meet you," Dante said through gritted teeth.

I looked at Elias through pleading eyes, silently begging him to take his hand. He did and you could see both men's veins protruding from their arms as they shook hands, trying to prove who was the strongest. Elias stayed quiet, not trusting the new man standing beside me.

"Dante, can you give us a second? I'll meet you at the car."

He was hesitant to move but nodded in agreement, leaving Elias and me alone. When Dante was finally out of earshot I let the rage of seeing Elias finally hit me and it hit me hard.

"What the fuck are you doing here?" I pushed Elias in the middle of his chest, he didn't move an inch.

"You know you could be nicer to me since I just helped you through a panic attack. Corvina I believe a thank you is in order.

Did this Dante make you forget your manners?" He crossed his arms over his chest.

"You keep his name out of your mouth. I'll ask you again one more time nicely before things get ugly. What are you doing here?" I was losing the little patience I had.

"Am I not allowed to enjoy myself Corvina? Is the great Corvina the only fae allowed to leave Aebriera and come visit the human realm?" His eyebrow arched.

"You hate humans, why would you bother coming here? Cut the crap, Elias." I rolled my eyes.

My pants pocket vibrated, a text from Dante.

```
You have five minutes before I leave you with your
new boyfriend.
```

These alpha males may be hot but they are both getting on my last nerve right now.

"You know I could turn you in if I wanted to. Your Mami has everyone in Aebriera looking for you."

I stayed quiet, knowing that if I goaded him that's exactly what he would do. Anything to get on her good side. Some things never change.

"I won't do that of course. If you can do something for me in return."

"Of course, can you ever do something out of the kindness of your heart? Oh wait, I forgot you don't have one."

"For my silence, I want one date." A smug smile now painted across his face.

"I would have to ask Dante if he's interested but I'm sure I can pull some strings for you. Didn't think he would be your type."

"Very funny Corvina. You know you're my type, always have been, and always will be." He kissed my cheek, walked back into the crowd, and disappeared into the night.

Chapter Nineteen

Dante didn't bother to look at me when I entered the car. As soon as my ass hit the seat he was zooming on home, he didn't even wait for me to put on my seat belt and I was looking forward to showing off my new skill. I was dying to say something to him but was struggling to find the words, breaking tension is not one of my strongest suits. My eyes focused on the road most of the drive, sneaking glances at Dante. His knuckles grew white from gripping the steering wheel so tight.

His anger was sucking out all of the air inside the car.

What right does he have to be upset? I was the one that was ambushed by my ex-fiancé!

So what if Dante and I almost kissed, he's not entitled to me. I don't belong to him, I don't belong to anyone and no one is entitled to me either. Those are the exact words that I told Elias the day I broke our engagement. The anger in me was building up, bubbling to the surface.

"Is there a particular reason that you look like you want to run us off the road?" I crossed my arms across my chest, trying to keep my composure.

"I'm fine." The sternness in his voice made the car feel ice cold.

It was suddenly so cold in the car that I was physically shaking. My fingertips felt frozen and I could see my breath as though it was the middle of winter. No cold air was coming out of the car vents, so where was this intense cold coming from?

"You can say you're fine all you want but your body language says otherwise. So how about you stop bullshitting me because I'm already in a crappy mood."

The car came to an abrupt halt, teaching me just how beneficial the seat belt is.

"I'm sorry princess. Are you in a crappy mood because of my presence? Would you like me to take you back to Elias?" Dante's words felt like venom.

My body felt like it was on fire, the cold now replaced by heat and if I didn't leave this car now I knew the damage I would cause would be disastrous. I unbuckled my seat belt to free myself, flinging the car door open. I heard his car door slam behind me as I swung open the shop doors. I ran up the stairs not wanting him to catch up to me. First, he lies, saying he's fine and now he has the nerve to snap at me when I'm trying to ask him what's wrong. I hate men that can't express their feelings, be a fucking adult.

Cabrón.

The apart door vibrated from how hard I slammed it shut. I sealed it shut with my magic, making it impossible for his key to work.

Fuck the no-magic rule right now.

Let Mami find me, I'll enjoy having an audience while I kick his ass. I am done with Dante Pendejo Cole. You could hear him fumbling with the key trying to unlock the door. I tried to breathe, to think calming thoughts, but right now all I can think of is how I want his obnoxiously beautiful head on a spike.

"What the hell?" Dante kept jiggling the door handle, as though it would loosen the door and allow it to open.

"Hey asshole, when someone locks a door it means to go the fuck away."

"Is asshole an upgrade nickname from Pendejo or?"

"Oh I'll tell you what an upgraded nickname is for you. Eres un imbécil y un maldito estúpido!"

"Okay, that does sound like an upgrade but it also doesn't sound good."

"Sounds amazing to me."

The door handle stopped moving and was replaced with a light tapping on the door.

"Morticia, please open the door. I'm sorry." Dante whispered.

I scoffed, thinking of all the times I'd heard that before. Men are only sorry once they witness a woman's rage over their stupidity. My power was trying to escape. The last time I was this upset, Papi had to get the entire west wing of our home rebuilt. I needed to get a hold of myself.

"Oh, you're sorry. Sorry for what Dante? Do you even know what it is you're apologizing for?" I screamed at the door.

There was no reply, only complete and utter silence from the other side of the door.

"That's what I thought," I mumbled under my breath.

A heavy sigh from Dante broke the silence. "I'm sorry for being a complete ass. Can you please open the door so I can look at you to give you a proper apology Corvina?"

"You don't get to call me that. Knowing and speaking my name is a privilege reserved for my friends. You, Dante Cole, are not my friend right now."

"I am your friend. A friend of yours that fucked up. Are your friends not allowed to make mistakes?"

Damn him, damn him for making sense.

I know the moment I open this door I'll see his stupidly beautiful eyes and forgive him even though I don't want to.

I opened the door. Dante started to make his way inside and I placed my hand on his chest, stopping him in his tracks.

"You said to open the door, you said nothing about letting you in. Now speak." I kept my hand firm on his chest.

"I own this apartment." He rolled his eyes.

"Are you going to apologize or do you plan to continue listing off all of the things that you own?" I put my hand on my hip, tapping my foot as my impatience grew.

"I'm sorry. I shouldn't have told you I was fine when I wasn't. Also, my Elias comment was unwarranted. Please forgive me. I was trying to protect you." His eyes were soft as he spoke and I could tell he was being sincere.

I closed my eyes, pinching the bridge of my nose as I took a deep breath.

"I accept your apology, only because it's been a long day. Listen to me when I tell you this. I don't need your protection. Not to bruise your manly ego, but I can protect myself better than you ever could."

He laughed and as he did I put my hands on his shoulder. My body turned as I stepped away from him pulling him towards me, making him lose his balance. I grabbed his arm as I placed my ass into his hips. I bent over, squatting as I pulled his arm making his body lift over me. I rolled him off of my hip as he flipped over and I knew that the impact to the ground knocked the wind out of him. I hovered over him, grabbing him by the throat for the second time today.

"This is the part where I would dig my nails into your throat and possibly rip it out but I'll spare you the pain since I've already proven my point." He gasped for air as I released my grasp.

"Lucky shot," Dante said in a raspy voice.

I reached out my hand as a peace offering. He grabbed my hand, yanking me down so I was now lying on the floor next to him.

"That was a dirty move, Dante Cole! This is the thanks I get for forgiving your poor behavior?" I said when I finally got the air back in my lungs.

He rolled over to his side, using his elbow and hand to prop his head up.

"I should've never told you my last name. You're going to abuse it now aren't you?" He rolled his eyes in annoyance.

"Absolutely. Don't get me wrong you're still my little Pen-dejo, but there is something about your full name. It just rolls off the tongue. Dante Cole, Dante Cole, Dante Cole."

I would've kept going but Dante rolled me on my back, his whole body hovering over me as he put his hand on my mouth to shut me up. He removed his hand quickly from my mouth when I bit him.

"That was a dirty move Corvina Morticia..." He was waiting to see if I would give up my last name.

"Nice try. Not happening." I flipped him over so that he was on his back and now my body was hovering his.

"You know I had to try. How do you know all of these fighting moves?" Dante was trying to move and failing miserably.

"My parents. Mostly my Mami, along with some of her friends. They're very into self-defense." I removed myself from on top of him, not bothering to reach my hand out again to help him get up.

"I wouldn't mind having a couple of lessons. If you could make time for me, I know you must have such a busy schedule." His voice dripped with sarcasm as he got off the floor and walked over to the front door.

"You want me to teach you how to fight. Why?" My eyebrows furrowed.

"Because you bruised my manly ego." He winked as he left the apartment.

Chapter Twenty

"**I**f I had a body like yours I would never wear clothes. I would get arrested on the daily from walking around the city butt ass naked." Holly whistled, causing everyone in the dressing room to spin their heads around to look at me.

I never had a problem with body image growing up, that was until puberty hit and then I noticed my thighs getting thicker, my boobs wouldn't stop growing, and my midsection went squishy. No matter how many diets or training sessions Mami would put me through my body refused to take a form other than thick. Holly noticed my shy smile and refusal to make eye contact. I started to shuffle back into the dressing room when Holly stopped me.

"I don't think so. Turn your ass back around."

I winced as I did as she told, hugging myself to cover my body.

"Come here," Holly motioned, beckoning with her hand.

I reluctantly followed her to the large golden-framed mirror hung on the wall. Holly stood next to me, her arms wrapped around me as she looked at me through the mirror.

"What do you see when you look in the mirror?" she asked.

"A woman whose body is trying to squeeze into a dress she has no business to be in."

"That's a shame. Do you want to know what I see?" she

asked.

"Not particularly."

"Wrong answer, Morticia. The correct answer is 'Yes, Holly you beautiful human I would love to know what's inside that lovely mind of yours.' Let's try that again." Holly looked at me, waiting for me to reply.

"Wait, you're serious? You want me to say that?" I asked and Holly crossed her arms in front of her chest.

I rolled my eyes. "Yes, Holly you beautiful human I would love to know what's inside that lovely mind of yours."

"Thank you for asking, Morticia. What I see is a beautiful woman wearing a stunning floral dress that hugs every one of her bomb-ass curves in all the right places. We always want what we can't have. As women, we get so caught up in what our bodies are 'supposed' to look like that we forget to appreciate what our bodies look like. Your body was made for you and only you. It's one of a kind, and that means it's special, so treat it as such and buy the damn dress."

"I wish I could've met your mother. She must've been an amazing woman to raise someone like you." I hugged her, squeezing her extra tight.

"She was pretty great, but I'm just speaking the truth. Now get your fine ass back into that fitting room and take off that so we can get lunch. I'm starving."

Holly smacked my ass as I walked away and I couldn't help but be grateful to the Gods to have a friend like her.

* * *

"Your ability to eat as much as you do and stay as tiny as you are is impressive." I sighed, stopping between the staircase steps to catch my breath.

Holly and I were starving after shopping. She recommended an all-you-can-eat Chinese spot. I had never had Chinese food before but wow that made me a fan.

"I thought I would have to roll you out of there. It's wild how you've never had Chinese food. Asian cuisine is easily on the top two in my list of things I love to eat."

"Thank you for helping bring everything up."

"Of course, I wasn't going to let you do a whole workout after eating all that food. You would've thrown everything up, I will not have you waste food like that."

Our laughter stopped abruptly as soon as I opened the apartment door. There Dante was, lounging on the couch, his feet crossed at the ankles and perched on the coffee table.

"Holly, call the cops. We have an intruder," I said.

"It seems like we do, and a messy one at that," Holly said, her face full of disgust.

I took a deep breath, trying to control my anger as I examined the crime scene. Not only were his disgustingly dirty biker boots on the table, but an array of junk food was spread out covering the living room table.

"You gave me shit about accidentally leaving a towel on the floor yet you can break in and leave a buffet for bugs?" I threw a bag of chips on his lap.

"First, it's not breaking and entering when you own the place, Princesa." He popped a chip into his mouth.

"Princesa?" Holly questioned.

"Long story," I said.

Holly shrugged her shoulders, sitting next to him, and grabbing a fistful of popcorn. I squinted my eyes at her, scowling her for joining the menace she calls her brother.

"Do not look at me like that. A show like this needs to be enjoyed with some popcorn." Holly shrugged.

"Second of all, I'm here to entertain you ladies." Dante pointed to the television.

Stars covered the screen and the words *A long time ago in a galaxy far, far away....*

Holly squealed, "Why didn't you just say we're going to watch *Star Wars*? Morticia hit pause on the fight please so you can see this masterpiece. I'm going to grab some blankets, can I borrow some comfy clothes?"

"Go for it," I told her.

She disappeared into the room and Dante patted the seat next to him. I stared him down as I took my seat, away from him.

"You wound me." He clutched his heart.

"You'll live," I said as I adjusted on the recliner closest to the TV.

Holly reemerged from the room, I couldn't help but laugh at her appearance. She was drowning in my clothes, her long red hair in a messy top not.

"Morticia, I don't wanna be a pain but I don't have my glasses. You mind switching seats?" She pouted her lips, making them quiver.

I dragged my body towards Dante, trying my hardest not to smack that stupid smirk off his face and keeping as much distance between us as possible.

"Everyone ready?" Dante asked.

Holly snuggled into her blanket, giving Dante a thumbs-up.

"Get ready to experience the best movie franchise ever," Holly said before Dante pressed play.

* * *

"How is it that Holly is always right?" I asked Dante as the ending credits of the third *Star Wars* movie scrolled on the TV screen.

"I'm not sure but it has to be witchcraft right? Do you want to watch another one?" Dante asked.

"It feels wrong if we keep going when she's passed out like that." I pointed towards Holly who was lightly snoring.

"Trust me she wouldn't mind, she's seen these hundreds of times. Plus, you do not want to wake the beast." As he spoke Holly rolled over, and he sighed in relief that he hadn't woken her up.

"It's okay, I'd rather wait for her."

"Anything else you wanna watch? Or would you rather I leave so you can read your sex books." Dante wiggled his eyebrows at me.

"I will not have you trash-talking what I read, especially when I'm unsure if you even know how to read. All these books are on *your* shelf, yet I have yet to see one in your hands."

"You're checking out my hands?" he asked.

"I hate you."

"No, you don't and I know how to read. I also know how to have sex so no manual needed."

I was about to scream when Dante put a finger over his mouth, reminding me not to wake Holly. "It's not a manual! It's about more than the sexy stuff okay, it's romantic. You wouldn't know romance if it bit you on your ass. Have you ever tried to read a romance book?"

"Nope." He popped the 'p' in the word as he spoke it.

"Well then, we're going to change that right now." I got up from my seat, making my way towards my room.

My books were scattered across the nightstand. I scooped

all of them into my hands, almost dropping them when Dante startled me.

"Sorry, figured it would be better to talk here while Holly is still snoozing."

"Pick one." I extended my arms so he could see all the books on display.

"I'm good thanks for the offer though."

"It's not an offer or a request. I'm telling you to pick one. Let me open your eyes to the world that is romance."

"Again, I don't need a manual."

"Come on, it's fun I promise. I trusted you when it came to baking, can you trust me with this?" I took a note from Holly's book, pouting my lips and making them quiver.

Dante rolled his eyes. "Fine. This one."

Dark romance. Oh, he's in for a treat.

"There you are young padawans. You had me worried. I thought you guys had been taken by the dark side." Holly rubbed her eyes and yawned as she stood at the doorway.

"I joined years ago little sis," Dante mumbled.

"What are you guys up to anyway?" she asked.

"Oh nothing, Dante is just picking up a new hobby," I winked at him.

Dante huffed before leaving the room, book in hand.

Chapter Twenty-One

The sound of my cell phone ringing woke me up the next morning. I reluctantly checked my screen and groaned when his name popped up.

I do not have the energy for his ass today.

I jabbed the decline button on my screen. It rang again and once again I pressed decline. I must've denied his call twenty times but he kept calling back incessantly.

Reminder to self; have Holly or Dante teach me how to block someone's phone number.

"You can't take a hint, can you? Stop calling me Elias!" I hung up the phone.

The phone rang once again, causing me to see red. I tried my best to answer it without snapping the phone in half.

"Still not a morning person I see mi amor." Elias' voice made my jaw clench.

"You're the last person I want to hear from so early in the morning, stop with the pet names before I take my blade to your tongue. The bliss of your silence would be overwhelming." My eyes are still heavy, wanting me to shut them and go back to sleep.

"You're breaking my heart with how quickly you've forgotten how special our mornings used to be. I have found it quite hard to forget how beautiful my name sounds when you're moaning it in my ear," he whispered through the phone.

"I highly suggest that you start speaking something of importance right now before I find a way to go through this phone to rip your face off," I growled.

"Always a flirt, I'm glad to see that hasn't changed. Now stop threatening me with a good time, it's distracting me from the purpose of my call. Be ready at 6:00 pm and wear that hot dress that's in your closet or the deal is off," Elias said and then quickly hung up the phone.

I stumbled out of bed, stomping my way towards the closet. There it was, hanging front and center. A floor-length sparkling scarlet red dress, the fabric was soft to the touch, even if there was little to no fabric. I hate how beautiful it is, damn him for having great taste. The dress was being held up by the tiniest of straps. The plunging neckline stopped right above the navel area and was accompanied by a thigh-high slit. I turned the dress around, shaking my head when I saw it was backless.

Putting on this dress would leave little to the imagination. The thought of being practically naked in front of Elias made my insides feel like they were on fire. Memories of our time together came back to me, making the room go hot and my underwear damp. My mind knew that he was no good for me but my body wanted nothing more than to have him devour me. Sometimes I loved our fights because I knew what would come after. He would shut me up with a passionate kiss, the kind of kiss that would leave you breathless. We would have a night that would include toe-curling, lip-biting, back-scratching, and everything else that would make any woman's night magical. It's a shame someone can be bad for you but feel so good. How cruel the Gods sense of humor can be. I slammed the closet shut, hoping those feelings stood with the dress.

My phone vibrated in my hand and I couldn't help but smile at the text on the screen.

```
"Woman! What the hell do you have me reading?"
"Haha. What part are you on?"
"He just cut someone's hands off because they groped
the girl he likes. How is this attractive?"
"It's called chivalry, Dante. You said you didn't
need a manual, but it sounds like you do. Take
notes. See you soon :)"
```

I giggled as I threw my phone on my bed, refusing to look at it again while I got ready for the day.

* * *

The shop was insanely busy and before I knew it Holly was flipping our sign around.

"Team Meeting!" Holly screamed as she locked the front door.

Dante rolled his eyes as we made our way towards the back of the store to grab a seat. Holly happily pranced her way in our direction.

"Tomorrow's bake-off day! It'll be great, I'll be there in my cheerleading uniform cheering you guys on!" Holly laughed as Dante gave her a look of desperation.

"For the love of God Holly please don't," Dante pleaded.

"Okay, fine I won't. But I do want to say thank you to you both for all your hard work. Especially Morticia for spending so much time with Dante, I know how rough that can be." Holly laughed as Dante ruffled the hair on top of her head.

"Shockingly enough, I've enjoyed it."

"Well, I'm glad to hear it! You guys can head out, I'll finish up here." Holly disappeared into the racks of clothing.

"There she goes again, flaunting that magic of hers," Dante whispered, making us chuckle.

It's an ongoing joke we have about Holly. She's always able to 'magically' disappear due to her small size. Holly eventually caught on and instead of being upset, she laughed, thanking us for making her feel special.

I've sensed no recent trouble. The visions have stopped since that night with Dante. It both worried me and brought me relief. The more I thought about my lack of visions the more I panicked, taking it as a bad omen. As Dante helpfully pointed out, I'm not a fan of silence. Silence means that chaos isn't too far behind.

"The king is dead and in his place has risen something far worse."

The Oracle's words have replayed in my head on a loop. I have to find a way to stop this coronation. Every plan that I've come up with has been a bust. The only way I can see out of this mess is to overthrow Mami and take my rightful place as queen.

"So how's your ego doing? Is it still badly bruised?" I gathered my belongings. Dreading that in a couple of hours, I will be with Elias instead of at the apartment cozied up with a good book.

"How kind of you to ask. It's healing up pretty nicely. Do you have anything planned tonight?" Dante leaned against the wall, crossing his ankles and stuffing his hands in his pockets.

"Actually, I do." Disappointment filled his face.

He lingered, waiting for me to elaborate. When I didn't he

cleared his throat.

"Okay. Well, I guess I'll see you tomorrow. Goodnight Princesa." He bent down, kissing me on the cheek goodbye before he left.

Of course, he wants to be sweet to me right before my date with Elias. I know this outing with Elias isn't a real date, yet it feels wrong that I'm hiding it from Dante. There is zero desire to spend time with Elias, especially when the taste of Dante's lips still lingers on mine, haunting me. A strong fragrance hit me as soon as I reached the apartment door.

Different bouquets were scattered, my feet crumbling the red rose petals that now covered the floor. An abundance of white and red roses, sunflowers, hydrangeas, peonies, tulips... the list goes on. In the center of the room was a vase full of golden blossoms with a white envelope sticking out.

Estoy emocionada de verte. Esperando que podamos empezar de nuevo.

– Besos,

Elias

The letter burst into purple flames in my hands, my magic burning it to a crisp. Elias' emotional state is none of my concern. Did he expect me to care that he was excited to see me and wanted to start from scratch? My only goal tonight is to play nice. Enough that it keeps him from outing my location to all of Aebriera. I have no interest in starting over a relationship that was doomed to fail. No matter how many flowers he sends my way it won't change the fact that Elias cares more about power than he does about me.

* * *

"Damn, I look good," I told myself as I looked at my reflection.

The hours spent in the bathroom getting ready were well spent. At first, I was going to give the bare minimum, because fuck Elias, but as I saw the dress hanging there I realized that it would be a disservice to the dress if I didn't look my very best while wearing it. My hair was now straight and parted in the middle, the length of it tickling my mid-back. Crimson red lipstick coated my plump lips, and my eyes popped from the black eyeliner painted on my lids. I made sure to make it as sharp as the blade that's nestled tightly on my right thigh right above the dress's slit. The teardrop earrings Elias included with the dress shimmered in the light as they dangled from my ears. There was a knock on my door as I fought with the strap of my heel. The shoe was perfect for this dress, honestly, everything Elias picked out for tonight was flawless and it made me hate him even more. The knocking continued and I abandoned the strap, letting it loose as I grabbed my purse to head to the door. I couldn't find my phone anywhere, I was digging through it when there was another knock on the door, making me roll my eyes at Elias' impatience.

"I'm coming!" I yelled at the door.

"Cabrón," I mumbled as I swung the door open.

My heart stopped when it wasn't Elias' face I was staring at but Dante's. His green eyes widened when he saw me, scanning every inch of my body and making me self-conscious of how much of it was currently on display. My arms found their way across my chest, trying to hide my breasts that were barely covered.

"I didn't mean to interrupt." His eyes glance over my shoulder.

"All you're going to see is an empty apartment. No one is

here." I moved my body out of the way to give him a better view, almost twisting my ankle as I did.

The flowers that previously took over the space were long gone. Dante shook his head, trying to convince me that's not what he was looking for, his attempt failed.

"I can help you with that." He pointed to my unstrapped heel.

"If you don't mind. That would be helpful. Thank you."

Dante bent down, his hand swallowed my ankle as he gently grabbed it to put my foot on his thigh.

"Did you need something from me, or is your sole purpose for this visit to help me with my shoe?"

He looked up at me as he looped my shoe strap into place.

"I made it all the way home before I noticed that this wasn't mine." He dug into his pocket, my phone looking small in his hand.

"Thanks, I was going crazy looking for this."

"No problem."

I couldn't help but stare at him, both of us in a frozen trance. It'd been minutes since he finished with my shoe, yet he made no signs of getting up.

"You look amazing by the way." His eyes were focused on mine.

I could tell he was trying hard to have his eyes focused, not wanting them to linger.

He's nervous and it's adorable.

I never thought that I would be able to have the same effect on him that he has on me. A male voice cut me off before I could thank him for the compliment.

"Saying she looks amazing is an understatement. I think she's the most stunning woman in all realms." Elias stood behind Dante, leaning on the stair banister with his hands inside his pockets.

Dante's body stiffened at the sound of his voice. Softly putting down my leg, he rose.

"Elias." Dante's voice was sharp and filled with hate, refusing to turn towards him.

My mind knew that I hated this male that was ruining this moment between Dante and me but my body was being a jerk and giving me butterflies. Elias looked like the definition of perfection. Wearing all black, the sleeves of his button-up were rolled up to his elbows. A gold watch hugged his wrist, making the tan of his skin and the veins in his hands stand out.

"Hello to you too, Dante. Would you so kindly make yourself scarce? You wouldn't want us to be late now would you?" He brushed his shoulder against Dante's, letting himself inside the apartment.

Whereas Dante tried his best not to look at me like a piece of meat, Elias had no such compunction. His eyes roamed over my whole body, reminding me of a predator ready to pounce on their prey. Elias bowed down, his lips grazing the top of my hand softly before kissing it.

"Mi Princesa. I will use the restroom while you say goodbye to your little friend." He dropped my hand, giving Dante a sideways glance before walking away.

Dante flinched as he heard his nickname for me come from Elias's lips. It was as though he had been smacked in the face.

I'm not his Princesa, I'm yours.

"Have fun." Dante's voice was monotone as he slammed the door in my face so hard the apartment shook.

I stood there, mouth agape. The thought of Dante thinking that this outing with Elias was anything of substance made my stomach go into knots. I opened the door, wanting to explain the situation to Dante but he was already gone. Just as I was getting ready to pull out my phone to text him Elias was at my side offering his arm to me.

"Thank the Gods he's gone. Now we can go enjoy our night." He playfully wiggled his eyebrows.

I scoffed at him, slapping his arm away.

"Why do you have to be such a dick?" I stomped down the stairs, the impact shaking the whole staircase as I descended.

"Why must you always pin me as the villain? He's the one that was at your doorstep when you were mine for the night. On his knees, by the way, I'm sure he enjoyed the view from down there. No doubt he could see right up that delicious dress of yours. He's the bad guy." He opened his car door for me and I rolled my eyes.

"Dante will never be the bad guy and you will always hate him for it. He's better than you in every way."

Elias raised his eyebrow as he asked. "In every way? I didn't realize he had you in every way, Princesa."

"Stop calling me that! You're disgusting and I am not discussing my sex life with you."

"Poor guy can't get it up, can he."

Oh, he can get it up just fine. I'll never forget how he felt under his jeans.

I stayed quiet, refusing to fall for his bait. Oh, what I wouldn't give to be able to punch that stupid smug look off of his face.

Elias' car screamed for attention. The exterior was a bright yellow with two doors that lifted when you opened them. The height of it was so low to the ground that I struggled to get into it, not wanting to expose myself in my dress. I jumped as my exposed back touched the cool black leather of the seat. There wasn't a scratch or speck of dust in sight. My body stiffened as Elias made his way into the car, all too aware of how small the inside of a two-passenger vehicle was. He made no effort to drive slowly, the car zoomed so fast that I was repeating a prayer to the Gods in my head. As expected the car ride was unbearable. Elias kept trying to make small talk. I gave him one-word replies, trying to make it clear that I had no interest in speaking to him, no matter how many questions crossed my mind about how he knew how to navigate the human world so flawlessly. My mouth stayed shut, knowing that he would see my line of questioning as an invitation to keep talking to me. I just wanted this night to be over so I could move on with my new life. The life where I was happy and that didn't include him in it.

Elias pulled the car into a brick driveway, in the middle was a fountain spouting out water and covered in dazzling lights. He parked in front of a gorgeous white house. Hedges lined the entire front of it, a pillar on either side of the red entrance door. A man dressed in a white button-down and black slacks approached my side of the car, opening the door for me to assist. I happily took his hand, silently thanking him for not trying to look up my dress as I exited the car. Elias gave the gentleman his keys as I smoothed out my dress.

"Have I told you how stunning you look tonight?"

"Yes," I said dryly.

"You have yet to compliment me on how I look. I guess that means I look too stunning for words."

"Are you feeling that insecure that you need me to tell you that you look pretty?"

Elias' face tightened and I felt my heart fill with glee.

"Where are we?" I asked.

I marveled at everyone around us, each person impeccably

dressed. The women wore colorful ball gowns accompanied by beautiful jewels while the men wore dashing suits. I breathed a sigh of relief, grateful for Elias' contribution to my outfit.

"It's a music gala to raise money for underprivileged children. They'll hold an auction where people bid money for items and the proceeds go to the children, giving them access to musical instruments and music classes." Elias shook hands with different men as we entered the house.

How does he even know these people?

"Be careful Elias, your heart is showing." I grinned at him and he laughed, walking us into the house.

"Oh mi vida. When will you learn that you are my heart?" He bent down and kissed my forehead.

Even in my six-inch heels, Elias towered over me. My face turned red, embarrassed by my body's betrayal of liking his lips on me.

I really need to cut back on my romance books, they're clouding my judgment.

"How does one get invited to an event like this?" I asked.

"I have my ways. I branch out to other realms now and again on your father's orders. Make connections, you never know when we will need allies."

Of course, always the perfect warrior for Papi Dearest. Elias left to get us drinks at the closest bar. My eyes widened, my brain finding it hard to process my surroundings, it was breathtaking. I've seen other faes eyes ogling my home when they visited, marveling at its beauty, but when you are so used to your surroundings you forget the beauty it holds to fresh eyes. The vaulted ceilings blinded me as I looked up at the multiple chandeliers suspended in the grand ballroom. All of the interior walls were a stark white, the only color coming from the paintings that were hung from gold frames on the wall. There was a history to them, they looked frail, as though if someone dared to touch them they would turn into dust. My phone chimed, and I had to resist the urge to reply.

```
"Wow. This is graphic. I'm trying to figure out how
these people are bending the way that they are. Is
this really what women want?"
```

I tucked my phone back into my purse. Dante does not deserve a text back from me since he wants to slam doors in people's faces. I felt a gust of wind behind me as Elias reappeared, champagne flutes in hand. I smiled as Dante crossed my mind. The memory of how he taught me about the different glasses in his cabinet and what alcohol is appropriate for each. I hadn't had the heart to tell him that none of this new knowledge would be put to use, I would forever chug straight from the bottle.

"Can you believe humans think this is art? If they ever saw our work back home they would look at this for what it truly is, garbage."

"You must be blind if you can't see the beauty in this, it's extraordinary. If there's anything I've learned during my time here, it's not to underestimate humans. They can surprise you." I sipped my champagne, its delicious taste coated my tongue.

"Oh humans are full of surprises, but there's nothing extraordinary about them," Elias scoffed.

Before I could argue with him a man's voice echoed through the room.

"Welcome everyone! Please grab your seat as the auction will start momentarily." The man speaking had a rugged look, handsome yet classy.

Elias led us to our table, his hand glued to my bare lower back. I was going to protest but decided against it when I noticed the men were ogling me. I'd rather deal with a monster I know than one who's unfamiliar. The last thing I need is to kill one of these men for touching me. He pulled out my chair, giving me a slight bow.

"You need to stop bowing. It's embarrassing!"

"Oh is Dante the only one allowed to get on his knees for you Corvina?"

"He was fixing my shoe."

"And I'm showing respect to my future queen."

"Did you miss the memo? Carmela is your future queen, not me."

"I beg to differ."

I emptied my flute, hoping that the buzz from the alcohol would make this night go faster. Suddenly my glass felt heavy in my hand, filled to the brim. I gasped when I realized it was refilled.

"You're welcome," Elias whispered.

"Are you crazy, don't use magic here."

"I will use my magic as I please."

I rolled my eyes, taking another sip of my drink. Should I make a game out of it? Take a snip every time I roll my eyes at him.

"Most of these people are too drunk or on drugs to notice." His hand gestured for me to observe my surroundings.

"You've made your point. Even so, there is no such thing as being too careful. There are rules put in place for a reason. You should know better, your Papi is the head of the royal guard."

"Exactly. Papi is, not me. I get more leeway." He pinched my perfectly blushed cheek and I smacked his hand away.

I'm going to need something stronger than champagne.

Where does one find the drugs that these people are on?

"My condolences about Castro." His eyes read of sorrow and I knew he was truly apologetic. He loved Papi just as much as I did, he was as much his son as I was his daughter.

"Thank you. Did you attend his burial? After all, you're the son he wishes he had. I think he was more heartbroken over our breakup than we were."

"Impossible. No one was more heartbroken than I was about you giving me back that ring." Elias slithered his arm onto the back of my chair, inching himself closer to me.

I cleared my throat, shimming myself as far off the seat as I could without falling off.

"It was beautiful and you were greatly missed."

I'm not sure why I asked, I knew he wouldn't have missed it. I shouldn't have missed it, but here we are.

Should I ask a waiter where to get the drugs? Are they serving them?

"I'm glad it was. He deserved the best burial Aebriera has to offer. I doubt that anyone noticed my absence."

My attention was now focused on the food in front of us. The aroma was delicious. A piece of steak covered in a beautiful sauce with mushrooms on top, paired with potatoes that smelled of the herbs that accompanied them and a side of vegetables. My stomach growled, alarming me that I was hungry.

"You were his world. His future queen." He finished his glass, immediately refilling it.

"I was his daughter and I wish that's all I was. Why can't Corvina ever be enough for anyone? My title constantly overshadowed me and I was sick of it." I sighed.

"Why is it that you see becoming queen as such a burden? It is a gift from the Gods."

"You see it as a gift because what you want most out of life is power. I see you for what you truly are Elias and that is a fae that wants to prove to his Papi that he is worthy of his love and because Clemente values power so do you and to a fault."

"That's not true and you will not turn this around on me." His eyes pierced into my soul, staring me down.

I grabbed my utensils and began shoveling food down my throat, hoping he would drop the conversation.

"Still good at deflecting I see." He sat up straight in his chair, digging into his food.

The auction began and so did the chaos. These bidding wars aren't for the faint of heart or the poor. All the prim and proper people that arrived became aggressive, cursing filled the room as people were outbid. How does one even acquire these massive amounts of money? Granted no item in the store was as luxurious as these: cars, paintings, tickets to sporting events, jewelry, vacations. The more money the people around me spent the more I drank. I'm no stranger to having unlimited funds back home, nothing was too expensive for me not to have, but now that I have to work to earn my money I don't spend it as frivolously as I used to. The last item was brought to the stage and immediately I was blinded by its beauty.

"Wow." I gasped. My elbow made its way onto the table as my hand cradled my head.

We had our fair share of jewels in Aebriera but something about this ring called to me. It was as though I needed to have it. The band was gold and resembled vines. In the center was a perfect pear-shaped emerald green jewel, on the sides of it were diamonds in the shape of flowers.

My hand flew to my mouth, trying not to spit out my drink as I heard the starting bid for the ring, $65,000. Elias chuckled, handing me a napkin to clean myself with.

"If this auction took place back home that would be mine in a heartbeat. I wouldn't even have to buy it, they would happily give it to me." I whispered.

"I thought you didn't want that type of power?" he whispered.

"I don't. I'm just saying it would've come in handy right now. Imagine how pretty it would look on my finger." I looked longfully at my hand, at how sad my bare finger looked.

"Excuse me, I'm going to head to the restroom." I could feel Elias's eyes staring at my ass as I walked away.

To my surprise Elias was behaving himself, it brought back memories from when he and I made sense. The days when we would stay up for hours talking. Or when he would surprise me by taking me out for picnics under our favorite tree, the same tree that still has our names carved into its trunk. We danced together, barefoot in the grass even though there was no music being played. I truly believed he was my forever, but it was all a lie. The perfect illusion and I was the perfect victim. Every word I said back there was true. Elias will never be able to love me in the way I deserve to be loved or make me feel the way I want to feel.

The way that Dante makes me feel.

I checked my phone and found my text from Dante.

```
I'm halfway through the book. I hate to admit it but
it's not that bad.
```

So he's into dark romance. Noted.

By the time I made it back to our table, the auction was over and they were directing people to a second room where dancing and more drinking took place.

"Aw, I missed it. Who's the lucky lady whose finger gets to be all shiny?"

Elias started to hand me my glass of champagne but retracted it, placing it on the table so he could catch me from stumbling over my own two feet.

"Not sure, I wasn't paying attention. I was worried about you. Did mi reina have too many glasses of champagne?" Elias' hands went from my arms down to my hands, his fingers intertwined with mine.

"Okay, do I need to give you a list of names you're not allowed to call me because I will. I'm not your queen and I'm fine. These stupid heels you had me wear are killing my feet."

It was only a half-truth. Maybe I did have too much champagne but it wasn't anything I couldn't handle.

"Are you using that as an excuse not to dance with me?" His hands were still intertwined with mine, giving them a quick squeeze, his silent plea for me to take him up on his offer.

"Just one song and then this night is officially over." I struggled to take off my heels.

Elias started to bend down just as Dante had and I stopped him. His mouth opened to object but he shut it quickly. He knew better. Any smart-ass remark would instantly have me change my mind about dancing with him. Finally, my feet were free and the shoes landed in the corner of the room never to be seen or worn again.

"Those were expensive cariño."

"You can add that name to the list."

My bare feet were suddenly in sandals that sparkled like the chandeliers above. Elias winked at me, his form of a thank you for me agreeing to his request. We made our way to the dance floor where a band played their hearts out, even though only a handful of people were dancing. We joined them in the middle of the room and as we did the the band filled the room with a slow-tempo song. Couples started to fill the dance floor, the women dragging their reluctant husbands. Elias pulled me into him, putting his arms around my waist as mine found their way around the back of his neck.

Elias and I shared plenty of dances at balls we attended together. All of this was second nature to us. We knew how each other's bodies moved and we did so immaculately, even after all this time.

"I missed this. You have to admit this feels right." Elias' hands made their way down the slope of my back, landing on my ass. I gave him a stern look, making his hands retreat.

"Please don't get swept up in the moment, Elias. This is pure muscle memory, there is no more us." I made it a point to look him right in the eyes.

"Remind me again why that is. What went so wrong that you can no longer stand my presence? Help me understand what doomed us." He tucked a piece of my straight hair behind my ear.

"Was what I said to you at the table earlier not clear enough? Or what I told you the day I gave you back that ring? Elias, you can't be that naive. You think you love me but you love the title that I have. The power and title you would obtain from marrying me." He lifted my arm, twirling me.

"I would be a fool not to acknowledge the fact that marrying you would mean I would be marrying a future queen. If you truly thought my love wasn't true then why accept my hand in marriage? "

He's right, why did I agree to marry him? The day he proposed filled my heart with joy, it was perfect. He asked using a family heirloom of his, the diamond ring shone in the sunlight and I knocked over our picnic as I tackled him to the ground, showering him with kisses. Of course, my parents were ecstatic, especially Papi. We were engaged for months after, but when I heard Elias and Papi talking about the future the ring started to burn on my finger.

"Maybe because I knew it's what Papi wanted, yet another rule for me to follow. Whenever I looked down at my finger, at that ring, I just kept replaying the conversation I heard between you and him. How you talked to him about me, felt more like a business deal than true love. Papi saw you as one of the fiercest warriors in his army, someone who would be strong by my side in a battle when needed. Fuck that. That's not what I want in a mate, in someone who is to be my partner. I want love. An unconditional love. A love that is pure, real, and doesn't care about any title. Elias, would you love me if I wasn't the heir to the Aebrieran throne?" I stepped away from him, wiping the tears staining my cheeks.

He stood there silent. That was all the confirmation I needed.

"This night is over. Take me home."

Chapter Twenty-Two

Elias sped his way back to the apartment and I was grateful that he could finally take the hint and didn't bother conversing. I felt no regret on my end. I meant every word that came out of my mouth with every fiber of my being.

I exited the car and stood on the sidewalk, waiting for him to say anything. He didn't, he looked defeated. I had never seen him this way.

Dammit. I can't leave him like this.

"Listen, Elias. I've been harboring so much anger towards you. I'm so tired of being angry. You will always have a place in my heart and our story will always be an important chapter of my life but that is all that it will be, just a chapter. Buenas noches Elias."

"Wait," Elias yelled, running to catch me before I went inside.

"I'm sorry. Please, take this as a gift of gratitude. It was a privilege to be yours even if it was just for a chapter." He pulled a ring box out of his pocket.

A bright light turned on inside the box as soon as he opened it, making the emerald ring shine bright in the darkness of the night.

"I can't accept this Elias. It's too much." I closed the box, clasping my hand with his.

"Of course you can. You've convinced yourself I don't love you, but you can't tell me how I feel. I know what I feel for you is real, whether you believe it or not Corvina."

"Maybe in another life, you would've been able to convince me that was true."

"I will want you in this life and the next. My heart will be yours in every life."

My heartbeat quickened as he removed my hands from his, reopening the box and sliding the ring onto my finger. Dammit, it looked just as amazing as I thought it would, the black polish on my nails making the emerald pop on my finger. The right thing to do was to take it off immediately, I knew it was wrong to keep it. If I kept this it would give him hope for our future. Elias placed his finger on my lips, silencing me before the words could exit my mouth.

"This ring is for you Corvina. Not for the princess of the Shadow Court, not for the rightful heir of the throne, just Corvina. Because you are enough, title or not, you've always been enough." His index and thumb fingers pinched my chin, keeping my face in place for him to look deep into my eyes.

"Come home with me. Come back and we can start over," Elias whispered on my lips.

Before I could compose a coherent thought his lips were brushing mine. Their softness and fullness consumed me. My body reacted to him like it always has, falling back into our rhythm of passion and hunger. Our kiss became ravenous as his teeth nipped at my lower lip and an involuntary moan escaped from deep in my throat. Elias' left hand grabbed my ass, while the other entangled itself to hair at the nape of my neck. He spun us around, pinning my body between his and the window of the shop. I could feel him harden as the kiss deepened. His fingers trailed my exposed thigh, making its way up the slit of my dress, ignoring the dagger and groaning when he realized that I wasn't wearing any underwear.

I hope he doesn't think that was for his benefit, underwear lines would've killed my outfit.

My body wanted to unravel, it had been so long since I felt his touch and now that I have it I don't want to let it go. As his lips touched my neck I snapped back to reality.

Why am I letting this man touch me?

My body is betraying me right now by trying to let him in. No, I won't. I refuse to be lured back into the wild vortex named Elias.

"I can't. Elias, this is a bad idea." I put my hands up, pushing at his chest to separate our bodies.

"Mi amor, I know you're more than capable. The things you do to a man are hard to forget." His lips grazed my ear.

"Another name to add to the list. Get your hands off me." I shoved Elias but he didn't budge.

"Elias, let me go. I'm not going to ask again." I growled under my breath, feeling my power rumble underneath my skin.

"I believe she asked you to let her the fuck go. Or should I forcibly remove you myself?" Dante appeared behind Elias, a murderous gleam in his eyes.

Chapter Twenty-Three

This is not going to end well. His hands were balled up in fists next to him, the rest of his body so stiff he could pass as a statue.

"Dante, I've got this."

"Listen to the beautiful woman that's underneath me and not you. She's not a damsel in distress. No hero is needed here, not that I would consider you hero material. You're more of sidekick material if that, so move along." Elias spoke to Dante without as much as a glance towards his direction.

"Oh, and you're hero material?"

"Your Papi thought I was. So did you once, or did you forget that Princesa?"

Dante strode towards Elias quickly but not quick enough. Elias' reflexes are one of an Aebriera warrior. Dante didn't stand a chance. He moved out of the way before Dante could get his hands on him. Dante looked me over, ensuring I wasn't physically hurt before giving his attention to Elias.

"Do not call her that." Dante fumed.

"You really wanna do this? You must love pain." Elias did what he was best at, being cocky and baiting his opponent.

"Funny, I was thinking the same thing," Dante said as he balled his right hand into a fist and swung.

Dante's fist met the air as Elias perfectly blocked his attempt to punch him.

"Is that all you got?" A mischievous grin grew on Elias' face, finding joy in Dante's rage.

"Can you two stop it!" I yelled as I placed myself between them.

"Like I said. She doesn't need saving. You're probably not used to the sounds a woman makes while she's experiencing pleasure. It's okay that you were confused." Elias puffed out his chest.

This was becoming ridiculous and I refused to let Elias play cat and mouse with Dante. We both know that Dante is no match for him, this would end in Elias pummeling Dante, which I won't let happen.

"Enough." I glared at Elias.

"No. This is what he wants right? To be your savior from the big bad Elias," he scoffed.

Elias charged at Dante and my feet stayed planted, refusing to move from my position. It didn't stop him, I was thrown to the floor. Elias threw an uppercut punch, hitting Dante's face with bone-shattering force. Dante stumbled back, balancing himself in time to not fall over. He rubbed his jaw, a bruise already starting to form. Elias smirked, admiring his work, and was unbothered by the fact that he knocked me to the floor. Dante's eyes were no longer green but pitch black as he noticed the blood that was trickling down my leg. I stumbled, trying to get back on my feet, wincing at the jolt of pain that went through my leg.

"You hurt her," Dante growled.

Elias looked my way and chuckled. He knew that my injury would be healed soon enough, I've experienced worse injuries during our sparring matches. Elias' chuckle was like lighting the fuse to a bomb. White light surrounded Dante as a chill hit the air. I could feel the magic radiating from him and the whole block shook.

"Are you doing this?" I ask Elias in a panic.

"I was about to ask you the same question." Elias fixed his fighting stance.

The power around Dante was building.

Oh, this is not good. He's going to...

I had no time to finish that thought. I quickly created a shield around myself, Elias wasn't as quick. Dante exploded and not in a figurative way. The magic slammed into Elias, knocking him off his feet and tossing him down the sidewalk. Elias' body was sprawled out on the cement, his clothing tattered up and his bottom lip busted.

"What the fuck?" Elias whispered.

How is this possible?

Dante dropped down to his knees, exhausted from using all that power. His body was still radiating white light. I ran, kneeling in front of him and grabbing his face. He was hot to the touch but I didn't care, burning myself as I inspected his body for any injuries.

"What's happening to me?" His voice trembled. Before I could answer I felt another surge of power, but it wasn't coming from Dante. Elias was running towards us and I could see the fury painted on his face.

"Over my dead body," I whispered

If Dante got to show off his magic, then so do I. My hands were engulfed in purple fire, bringing them together to fashion a whip. I lifted my right hand above my head, swinging it in the air before flinging it towards Elias, tripping him and knocking him off his ass.

I've still got it.

Before he could get back on his feet I ran towards him, grabbing the dagger from my thigh. My foot hit his chest, making sure he stayed down as the dagger grazed his throat.

"Make one more move, Elias, and the Gods will be welcoming you with open arms." I pressed the dagger harder into his skin, blood running down his throat.

"Did you know he could do that? Who the fuck is he? No, what the fuck is he?" The dagger drew more blood as his throat moved.

"None of your fucking concern. You need to go back home and not come back. We made a deal and I've paid up. Stay truthful to your word." Carefully I removed my dagger from his throat. He opened a portal and disappeared without saying another word. I wiped the dagger on my dress, removing Elias' blood, before making my way back to Dante. He was still on his knees, unable to move.

"Now, what to do with you, Mr. Dante Cole?"

Chapter Twenty-Four

"What the fuck is going on Morticia? How did I just? And you just..." Dante was finally able to lift himself from the ground.

"Dante, I need you to calm down. I can explain everything, I need you to breathe. The last thing I need right now is your emotions to get the best of you. Gods forbid, you explode again." His head was gripped between my two hands, forcing him to look me in the eyes.

Dante's breathing finally started to steady. He intertwined his fingers with mine as I dragged him to the apartment. His body was stiff as he sat down. I tried handing him a glass of water but he didn't move.

"I exploded?" he asked.

I know he is so confused right now and I shouldn't think this is adorable, but it is.

"Yes, you did. Dante does anything hurt?" My eyes scanned his body looking for any sign of injury.

He just shook his head no in response. His eyes widened as they scanned my knee, noticing all that remained from my injury was dried blood.

"I'm going to tell you something and I need you not to panic. Can you promise me to do your best to stay calm for me?"

He nodded.

"Okay, good. Magic is very fickle when it comes to emotions so please stay as calm as you can. Everything I'm about to tell you is completely true and about to open your eyes to a whole new world." His hand was ice cold but I refused to let it go, hoping it would help ground him.

Again he just nodded in response as I took a deep shaky breath.

"My full name is Corvina Morticia Umbra and I'm not from this realm. I'm fae. My home is a land called Aebriera and when you met me I was running away. Castro Umbra is my Papi and he is the most powerful dark fae king our realm has ever known. I am the sole heir to his throne, which is something I don't want." I paused, giving Dante time to digest the information.

"You're a fae princess?" He questioned.

"Well, when you put it that way it doesn't sound that impressive." I shrugged, trying to lighten the mood.

Dante stayed silent.

"Yes, I am. I'm sorry for hiding that part of myself from you and Holly. Please hear me when I say that you must not tell anyone about me, that includes Holly. I don't want either of you in danger." I tightened my grip on his hand, scared he would pull away.

"Why would we be in danger?"

"Because of people like Elias who work for the royal guard. They want me home and I don't think it's for a family reunion."

"Is Elias also fae? You guys met and dated in that world?" Dante's eyebrows furrowed.

"It's called Aebriera and yes, he is. We were to be married before I called it off." My eyes glanced down, realizing that the ring he bought me earlier tonight was still on my finger.

Dante's voice once again disappeared, nodding in response. He wasn't scared of me, but would he accept me?

"My life is complicated, Dante. I love my family but I couldn't be the queen my Papi wanted me to be, what my people need me to be. Now he's gone and Mami will be crowned because I'm not there to claim the throne."

Dante's eyes softened. "Gone?"

"He passed while I was here." I looked away from Dante as the shame overtook me.

"I'm sorry." He removed his hands from mine, rubbing my back to console me.

This wasn't the time for a breakdown, but as Dante rubbed my back it hit me that I never got to say goodbye, stupidly concerned about what would happen if I returned home and not thinking about the repercussions my heart would endure.

"I didn't go home. Oh, my Gods, I didn't go home and he's gone. I have to live for centuries with the guilt of him dying and I wasn't there to say my goodbye." I sobbed as Dante held me, my chest felt constricted like I couldn't breathe.

"You live for centuries?" Dante whispered, the lightheartedness of his question made me burst into laughter.

"Yes, I do. I also heal fast, hence." I pointed at my knee.

Dante rubbed his thumb across it, the dried blood crumbling from his touch.

"Seeing you hurt..." Dante whispered.

"I'm okay now. Thank you for defending me."

"Even though you didn't need me to?"

"Even though I didn't need you to."

"You know I always will though right?"

"I'm sure you will, you stubborn Pendejo."

Dante chuckled and it was like music to my ears to hear him

laugh again.

"Enough fae fun facts. We have to figure out what the hell you are. Hate to break it to you Mr. Cole but there is no way that you're human." I crossed my arms across my chest.

"So what I did down there was because of magic?" He asked.

"Oh yeah, and it was powerful stuff. I told you my whole truth now it's time to tell me yours." My eyebrow arched.

"I have never experienced anything like that in my life, trust me that's something I would remember."

"What were you doing here so late at night anyway?" I asked.

"I couldn't sleep so I figured I would do some baking at the shop." He bit his lip, stopping himself from saying more.

"Hmm... and this had nothing to do with the fact that I was out with Elias tonight?" I gave him a knowing glance.

" You weren't replying to my texts. I just wanted to make sure that you got home safe. Plus I felt like a dick just walking out on you like that and I wanted to apologize."

"Two apologies in the same week. You're on a roll."

"I swear I am done with being an ass for the rest of the week. Cross my heart and hope you don't die. That saying feels a lot heavier now, knowing everything I know."

We both burst out into a fit of laughter, laughter that we both desperately needed.

"You better be, we have work to do. You just had to show off your magical powers to me huh? I forgive you, but only because I'm scared that if I don't you'll explode on me next and I very much like being in one piece."

He playfully shoved my shoulder and my heart couldn't help but flutter. Even though I never needed his protection he was willing to offer it anyway out of the goodness of his heart and not to show off his dominance to another male or to impress my papi like Elias had done time and time again. It was for my well-being because he cared about my safety.

"Thank you for sharing with me. I understand why you didn't tell me. If I didn't see it with my own eyes I would think you were crazy. I'm glad there are no more secrets between us now." Dante's smile broke me.

No more secrets between us. Except for the fact that I erased a part of his memory.

"To answer your text from earlier, yes that is what women want," I smirked and Dante laughed.

"I'm going to have to do some stretching then."

"Yeah, do me a favor and stretch on your own time. I do not want to see that."

"Mentirosa," he whispered.

"Okay, where did you learn all these Spanish words? I'm not a fan."

"Sure you don't."

He's right, you are a liar. You love it.

"Ex-fiancé huh? Didn't think you were the marrying type," Dante said.

"Ouch." I put my hand on my chest, right where my heart was.

"I just mean, well you confuse me. You read romance books for fun yet when I've talked about love in the past you said 'fuck love, there's way more interesting things to talk about.' So which is it Corvina? Do you only accept love if it's written on paper?"

"I'm a complex creature, Dante. What can I say." I shrugged.

"What do we do now and why do I feel so exhausted?" Dante yawned.

"Well you said you couldn't sleep, now you'll sleep like a

baby. You exerted a lot of energy and that amount of power you released is bound to drain you. Go home, rest and we'll figure it out tomorrow morning." I smiled, his droopy eyes showed me just how tired he was.

I found myself sweeping Dante's hair away from his face, his usual bun had unraveled in the chaos. He went head to head with an Aebrieran warrior and all he received was a light bruise. I lightly grazed it and he smiled at me lazily, as though it took all his strength.

"Does it hurt?"

"Not at all." His hand met mine, his thumb caressing it to ensure he was alright.

A part of me is relieved that Dante isn't human. I don't have to hide from him anymore but I can't help but be scared for him.

"Shit." Dante sighed.

"What's wrong?"

"I just realized, tomorrow is the bake-off." The palm of his hand dragged in front of his face.

"Shit indeed." I bit my lip as I began to think, trying to find a way that we could both not compete without Holly wanting to murder us both.

"She'll kill us if we don't make it." Dante sighed as he got up.

"My thoughts exactly. We'll compete, kick some ass, and then we can have our focus on what's going on with you and your explosive tendencies."

"What if it happens again and we're in public this time? I don't want to hurt anyone."

"You won't. I'll make sure of it. Plus, I've worked my ass off to produce something edible. We're doing this!"

Dante nodded his head in agreement.

CHAPTER TWENTY-FOUR

"You think I could be more powerful than you?" He teased me.

What if he is?

"Oh, you wish." I nudged him.

"Holly fucking owes us one and she doesn't even know it." He shook his head as we walked over to the front door.

"Our little secret Dante, for now. I promise we can tell her one day but for now, it's too risky." I opened the door to let him out.

"I know, I know. Cross my heart and hope you don't die. Goodnight, Princesa. The nickname is less fun now that I know you're an actual princess."

"So you're going to stop calling me that?"

"I said it was less fun, not that the fun has completely disappeared."

Why did a wave of relief just hit me? Oh yeah, because you love the butterflies Dante gives you whenever he calls you Princesa.

He started to speak but before he could I cut him off, placing a hand over his mouth.

"Don't you dare try to learn the Spanish word for Queen! Try it and I will not hesitate to hurt you, powers or not." I released the grip I had on his mouth.

"Heard you loud and clear. Goodnight, Ms. Umbra." He smirked, closing the door before I could reach out to strangle him.

Chapter Twenty-Five

What does one wear to a bake-off?

I rummaged through the closet, trying to answer that question. The clock was ticking, Dante would be here any minute. I threw on a pair of ripped jeans, sneakers, and a graphic t-shirt that Holly gifted me. She said, "I knew you had to have it." I had just finished painting on some lip gloss when Dante did his usual knocking before letting himself in.

Magic or not, some things never change.

"I'm in the bathroom, I'll be right out."

As I stepped out of the bathroom I scanned the living room looking for Dante, finding him in the kitchen taking inventory of his wine collection.

Like I said, some things never change.

"Are you ever going to stop taking inventory? Don't you trust me?"

"Nope. Never. Nice shirt by the way."

"Holly said it was 'so me' but honestly I have no idea what it means."

"She's not wrong. Especially since I've experienced firsthand what type of books you read." He smirked.

"Since we're on the topic, are you done with the book I let

you borrow? If so I would like it back."

"I'll let you know when I'm done. I'm reading it at my own pace."

"Yeah painfully slow."

"I'm sorry that I haven't had the urge to read your sex book after finding out that I have magic." Dante flailed his arms

"Drama queen. So are you going to explain the shirt to me or are you going to continue to be a pain in my ass?" My Dante annoyance meter was starting to reach peak levels.

"It says 'Give me smut or give me death'. You're essentially wearing a shirt that says you'd rather die than read a book without sex."

My face turned bright red. "I'm changing right now."

"No, keep it on. It'll intimidate the other contestants. You'll get dirty looks from parents but we're already running behind and Holly will kill us if we're late."

Against my better judgment, I listened to Dante and kept the shirt on.

"Are you ready to kick some ass, Umbra?"

"Have I told you lately that I hate you, Cole?'

"Actually, no. You've never told me that."

"Hmm, I guess I've been keeping that an inside thought this whole time. Shocking that I was able to keep that one to myself." I giggled but the laugh was cut short, interrupted when Dante opened his mouth, speaking words that broke my heart.

"That's fine. Hate me all you want. People that hate me don't get any of my baked goods. Nothing I bake will ever touch your lips again," he said with an evil grin.

"You're evil. That is the cruelest thing you've ever said to me. Take it back!" I playfully slapped his arm.

"I'll take it back when you take back that you hate me."

"Fine. I'll take it back." My monotone voice was very unconvincing.

"Say it like you mean it. I need to hear you say it, Princesa." Dante arched his eyebrow, crossing his arms as he waited for me to cave in.

"You know I could easily force you to make cookies for me." I allowed a purple flame to engulf my hand but he knew it was an empty threat.

"I am well aware of your magical abilities. Now take it back. Or is the powerful Corvina Umbra unable to admit that she can't live without me?"

"Okay! I don't hate you, Dante. Now that I think about it, you're the light of my life and my world is better with you in it." I said begrudgingly.

"Now, was that so hard?" He pinched my cheek with a smug look on his face.

As he looked at me, I processed my words and everything clicked. I spent years thinking the love Elias gave me would be the best I'd get. Dante has proven me wrong in so many ways. The way Dante's touch sent chills down my body. How the sound of his voice soothes me. Even his stupid jokes made my day. I can tell him I hate him all I want but it would be a lie. If I'm honest with myself there's not a thing about this man that I despise. His smile, how he takes care of his sister, how he took me in without even knowing me because he could tell I was a lost soul that needed help. He stood up for me even though he knew I didn't need his help.

Holy shit, I'm in love with Dante Pendejo Cole.

Chapter Twenty- Six

I hadn't realized how many people would attend this event and my nerves made me want to puke. Dante grabbed my hand, using his thumb to caress my palm. I gently pull it away, trying to put distance between us.

I love him.

I don't know when it happened but it did. Denying it won't make it any less true but I have to deny myself the luxury of his touch, because having it means I will only want more. I thought it was just a physical attraction, how the fuck did this happen so quickly? There are a million reasons that Dante and I wouldn't work, I counted all of them on the car ride here. I still have no solution to stopping Mami's coronation other than taking the crown myself. I've been dreading having to tell him that I have to leave.

A great white tent was set up in the middle of the bright green grassy field. There were hundreds of booths, each offering different services and items for sale. As soon as we stepped into the tent Dante's eyes glimmered. There were rows of ovens and stoves, all in pristine condition. All of the bakers were admiring the setup, their eyes twinkled just as Dante's did as they played with their new toys. Hanging above each station were large signs with the names of the bakeries, making it easier for the contestants to find their stations. Dante and I didn't need any assistance finding ours, I'm not sure how Holly did it but our sign seemed much larger than all the others. There she was under it, waving her hands in the air frantically. She wore one of the biggest smiles I've ever seen. If you didn't know Holly you would think that she was just excited for the event and that this wasn't the energy she radiates daily.

"There you two are!" she squealed, throwing herself at us.

"I got you both a gift!"

Two beautifully light blue wrapped boxes sat on the counter, a beautiful gold ribbon on top. My heart felt so full as I admired the wrapping, knowing Holly spent time on them herself. I popped open my box and couldn't help but burst out in laughter. Tears started to blur my vision as my laugh became uncontrollable. Dante held up his gift as he gave Holly a death glare.

"I'm not wearing this," he snarled.

Holly had bought us new aprons to wear as we baked today. Mine was a cream color and had gold glitter writing on the front that read *The Beauty* on the front of it. Holly had gifted me one of her favorite childhood stories, *Beauty & the Beast*, and I had fallen in love with it. Dante's apron was the reason for the tears rolling down my face as he grimaced, holding it up to his body. A crisp white apron that read in a bright red font *The Beard* with a picture of a bearded man right under the wording. When I could finally catch my breath I thanked Holly for my gift, wrapping it proudly around my neck and tying it at my waist.

"Come on Dante, don't be a bore, put on your apron." I snickered.

"Be grateful! It was between this or *Kiss the Baker*. But I doubt

Morticia would want to stare at that all day." Holly winked at me and my face turned red.

Nope, I wouldn't want to be tempted to kiss the man I love all day. Not more than I already am, anyway.

"You're lucky I love you, Holly." Dante hesitated before tying the apron around his waist.

"As if you have a choice. I'm impossible not to love." She flipped her hair before disappearing into the crowd.

Dante's eyebrows were furrowed, frustrated by the little human he called his sister. I flashed him a huge smile, trying to look as innocent as possible. My hand reached out grabbing his right cheek hidden under his thick beard, pinching it between my thumb and index finger.

"Now, was that so hard?" I chuckled.

Dante reached over the counter, grabbed some flour, and tossed it at me.

I coughed as the white powder entered my lungs. "You do not want to start a food fight with me. Especially when I don't need to use my hands to throw things."

He waved a white rag in front of us in response.

"Are you ready for this?" he asked.

"I think so. Unfortunately, my teacher was pretty mediocre but we should be fine." I dusted off the flour that was sprinkled on my apron.

"What a shame. I'm sure he'll be heartbroken to hear your review because he thought you were a great student." Dante walked past me, gathering everything we might need before the competition began.

"Can I ask you a question?" The words slipped out of my mouth before I could stop myself.

"Technically that is a question. But sure, shoot." He leaned against the oven, crossing his feet at the ankles.

"Have you had a lot of other students before me?" I start biting my nails, regretting asking the question as soon as I see Dante's face drop.

Smooth move, Corvina. Ask the man you have feelings for if there were other women before you. Of course, there were I mean look at him.

"Uhm, no. There was one person before you, but that was a long time ago." He shrugged his shoulders.

"What happened to them?"

Dante paused, rubbing the back of his neck. I could tell he was having an internal struggle, debating if he wanted to answer.

If he wanted to tell you he would. Don't force the man to let you in.

"Don't worry about it. It's none of my business, I'm not sure why I even asked." I opened a drawer next to the oven, wanting to hop inside it and never come out.

Instead, I find the utensils we'll need to use. I put them on the counter, trying to ignore the deep stare that Dante was giving me. The whisk slipped out of my hands, landing by Dante's feet. I bent down to retrieve it and as my hands grabbed it so did Dante's. Electricity shot up my arm, reminding me of the first time we ever had physical contact. I let go immediately, leaving the whisk in his hands.

"I don't mind telling you, Corvina." He placed the whisk in the sink across from us.

"Her name was Adeline. We were together for three years. I'd never taught a girlfriend of mine to bake. Honestly, no one before her was interested enough to learn. She was a natural at it, we won every year." He paused and as he did I knew exactly what was happening in his head. He was reliving memories.

It was a jab to my heart with every compliment I heard him give Adeline. Dante's entire face was beaming with love as he spoke about her but his eyes were also full of sadness.

"I knew her my whole life. She was our next-door neighbor. One day she showed up to say hi and she never left. We were friends at first until one day it just happened." Dante cleared his throat before continuing.

"The apartment you're staying at used to be ours. One night I went out for a run to clear my head. Adeline and I were fighting right before she went out with some friends. I tried calling and texting her, wanting to apologize, I can't even remember what the fight was about. There was a loud crashing noise, I followed it and a car was up in smoke. One of the cars was completely flipped upside down and you could see the gas gushing out from the tank. The closer I got the more my heart started racing, it was Adeline's car." Dante's knuckles went white as he tightly gripped the oven handle.

"She was unconscious and I kept yelling her name over and over again trying to get her to wake up. The window was already shattered so I reached for her, cutting up my arms in the process."

He looked down and there they were. Little scars that I never noticed before today.

"I was able to undo her seat belt but her feet were pinned in, I couldn't get her out. I called the police and heard someone moan in pain from behind me, his head had a big gash on the side of it that was oozing out blood. It was obvious that he was the other driver, I yelled at him to try to help me get Adeline out but he just started vomiting and that's when I started to smell it. The douche-bag was fucking drunk, he was drunk and he got behind the wheel. I was going to go over there to give him a piece of my mind but that's when I felt fingers brushing my hand. It was Adeline, she had finally woken up." Tears started to form on Dante's face. I rubbed his back, trying to console him the best I could.

"Sometimes when I close my eyes all I can see are hers staring back at me. The fear that she must've felt. She knew she wasn't going to make it. She kept begging me to leave her once she smelt the gasoline, but I couldn't. What kind of man would I be if I left her there to die? It wasn't until she mentioned Holly and how I couldn't leave her alone in this world that I found the strength to leave. That's the only reason I left. She told me how much she loved me. I told her that I loved her too but she had to tell me how much she loved me again once she was safe. Sirens were blaring as I stepped away from the car, watching as Adeline slowly slipped away, praying that they would come in time to save her. But they didn't. The car exploded before they had the chance to try and save her. That explosion shattered my heart into a billion pieces." He sighed deeply, sniffling back his tears.

I learned the hard way a long time ago, that even magic can't heal a broken heart.

"I'm so sorry Dante."

"Remember when I told you that there was someone in the French bakery that I didn't want to see?"

I stayed quiet, giving him a single head nod as a response.

"That someone was the man that caused the accident. He was found guilty but only sentenced to one year in jail. One year is supposed to be enough retribution for his crime. He took away the love of my life. It took everything in me that day not to walk across that bakery and kill him."

"I can imagine. Vengeance is a strong feeling." Tears started rolling down my face.

Dante looked at me, brushing away my tears.

"I've wanted vengeance for a long time, but that's not what Adeline wouldn't want for me. She wouldn't want me to feel angry about what happened. Adeline didn't have a hateful bone in her body, even while she was dying she accepted her fate and she wanted me to accept it too. I'm grateful for the time we had together. Yes, I use the apartment to escape Holly, but I also feel close to Adeline when I'm there. I would sit there and think of the memories we shared, it was my safe place to cry and feel like she was next to me. That day I saw you in the alley, I swore I could hear Adeline tell me to take you in. Actually, it felt more of a threat. 'If you don't help that poor girl so help me God Dante'. That's the kind of person she was, constantly helping those in need, so I helped you."

I wrapped my arms around his waist, his body enveloping mine and I sunk into him. Forget about keeping myself distant. I need Dante to see that I care about him, for him to feel how sorry I was that he ever had to feel that kind of loss. He experienced the type of love I've been craving and lost it all.

Why must the Gods be so cruel?

He caressed the top of my head, kissing my forehead.

"Are you ready to bake now?" Dante asked.

"Yes. We're going to bake our asses off, for Adeline." I looked up at him, watching him catch his breath.

"Thank you," he said before we finished getting ready to bake the best damn cookies of our life.

Chapter Twenty-Seven

How can someone be so excited about second place? Holly was jumping up and down like we carried gold medals instead of silver ones. To our demise, the French bakery won.

The silver metal, designed to look like a chocolate chip cookie, hung around my neck. Who would've thought a hunk of metal would be my new most prized possession?

"Let's go celebrate!" Holly was buzzing with so much excitement I thought she might explode.

I cannot handle another Cole sibling exploding on me right now.

Dante and I gave each other a knowing look, both nodding in silent agreement.

"One drink, Holly, that's it." Dante gave her a stern look, which Holly ignored as she pecked him on the cheek.

* * *

Our mini-celebration turned into a bar-hopping celebration, causing Dante and I to try to sober up in the apartment. That girl is tiny but man can she out-drink us both. We tucked Holly into my bed to sleep it off.

"How did we let this happen?" Dante chugged water.

"Are you sure Holly doesn't have any magical abilities? I'm pretty sure she has the power to convince people to drink way more than they should." My head was already pounding.

I took a huge bite out of a cold slice of pizza I found in the fridge.

"As soon as Holly leaves we can get to work." Dante snatched my pizza crust from my hand, winking as he did.

"We don't have to wait." I gave him a mischievous smirk.

Before he could ask I quickly opened a portal, shoved him inside it, and followed right behind him. Holly would be asleep for hours, she wouldn't notice even that we were gone. I need the answers and I need them quick before I leave for the coronation. Dante froze in shock as he took in his surroundings, an area that I knew like the back of my hand. It was cloudy and lightning lit up the sky, even with a storm rolling through my Aebriera was beautiful. The grass was beautifully green and went on for acres, the trees swayed in the wind and their leaves were a mixture of green and brown. The mud under my boots sloshed as I walked my way towards Dante. Smiling as my brain shuffled through my memories of Papi and Mami bringing me here, teaching me everything I know about my powers and fighting. Normally this arena would be buzzing all year round but with the coronation just around the corner, all hands will be on deck and no one would be concerned about training right now. Dante taught me about baking, now it's my time to be the teacher.

"Corvina... holy shit." Dante's mouth was gaped open.

"Close your mouth before something gets in there." I chuckled as I forced his mouth shut.

"This is a mock battlefield that my court uses for training and it's where I'll be training you. Granted there's only so much I can show you in such a short time but I want you to be able to defend yourself without needing to blow up every time you use your powers."

"Defend myself from who or what exactly?"

"The possibilities are endless in a land of magic. This can be a place of beauty but it also holds horrors."

"So this is Aebriera?" Dante twirled a piece of grass in his hand.

"Yes, more specifically the Shadow Court. This field is a couple of miles away from my home."

"So teach, where do we start?" Focus and determination filled his eyes.

"Let me bruise your manly ego a little more." I took a fighting stance.

"I'm so happy no one is going to be around to see this shit show."

Dante sighed as he took his sloppy fighting stance.

Well, there's lesson number one.

* * *

"Again," I yelled at Dante.

"Corvina come on, can we take a break?" Dante panted, sweat dripping down his face.

"You think your attacker will let you take a break?" I swiped my leg under Dante and down he went.

I pounced, grabbing both his wrists in my hands and placing my full body weight on top of him. "You wanted a break, here's your break. Now you're flat on your ass because you couldn't properly defend yourself from me. Familiar feeling isn't it? Feels right if you ask me."

Dante bent his hips, bringing his legs up. His left leg was now in front of my face and he rocked forward. He used his leg across to drive down towards the ground, forcing me to roll onto my back. His fingers intertwined with mine as he hovered above me, successfully pinning me to the ground.

"I like this feeling much better, Princesa," Dante whispered.

"I've been in the shadows for hours watching this catastrophe. I refuse to watch any longer." The Oracle stood right behind Dante, scaring him half to death.

Dante quickly recovered. He positioned himself into the new and improved fighting stance I taught him a a mere hour ago.

No bad. Maybe I should be a teacher instead of a queen.

"Always so sneaky." I hugged my friend.

"Stand down pendejo. She's a friend."

"A friend? More like her only friend but yes. Hello, it is I." The Oracle snickered and Dante made no sign of moving.

"So this is Dante Cole. A pleasure." The Oracle hovered around Dante, making him visibly uncomfortable as she circled him.

"Uhm, hello. Yes, that is my name, and you are?" Dante refused to make eye contact.

Oracles refuse to reveal their names to outsiders. They prefer to be seen as a whole, not as individuals, they try to protect their kind as much as possible. It's why I feel so honored to know hers.

She nodded and I smiled, she trusted us.

"Veda. Her name is Veda and she is an Oracle. She has powers that might help us figure out who you are, and where you came from. I know this is a lot to digest. We are in a bit of a time crunch but we can wait if you're not ready."

Dante cut me off. "I need to know."

"Is it okay if she touches you?"

He nodded his head.

Veda grabbed his hands, the iris of her eyes disappearing and going completely white, moving side to side as she searched. Her sight took her between his past, present, and future, taking in all the information the Gods would grant her. Dante's eyes were locked on mine, unsure if he should be looking at Veda as she worked. She gasped before letting go of him.

"It's you." She stepped back, mouth agape.

Veda kept one of her hands gripping Dante's and took another to grab mine.

"Let me show you."

A baby. A beautiful boy who is being carefully held by a beautiful fae. Her chestnut brown hair is long and wavy, and next to her is her husband looking at them both lovingly with his beautiful piercing green eyes. Across from them stood an oracle.

"He will be powerful. The power he'll possess will be so great that Castro will come looking for him when he finds out about his existence. You must get him away from here, hide him! He will find his way back to you, I promise."

The oracle opened a portal, urging them to go through. They held the child, crying as they kissed him and said their goodbyes.

"Mommy and Daddy love you, Salvatore. We must have faith to do what must be done. You're going to do amazing things and we cannot wait to hear about your adventures in this realm. We'll be waiting patiently for you to return to us."

They laid him in a woven basket and placed it in front of a door. The mother gave her baby one more loving look before knocking gently on the door. Both of them disappeared back into the portal before the door opened. Flashes of Dante's childhood came to me: His adoptive parents bringing him home, his first day of school, his visiting Holly when she was born in the hospital, his first kiss, the day he met Adeline and the day he lost Adeline. She was beautiful. Seeing them together brought me joy rather than a raging jealousy. My heart is full, knowing that he experienced true happiness, and because of her, he knew what true love is. The next set of flashes were more recent memories: the day that I met him and Holly, us reading the comment cards, preparing for the bake-off, our research and us making out in the kitchen.

I pulled my hand from Veda, breaking our connection.

No.

"Wait, what was that last part? That didn't happen. Show it to me again." Dante asked Veda.

"Please don't," I begged her.

"I am here for the truth Corvina, Not to keep things hidden." Veda gave me a look of shame.

She shook her head, giving in to Dante's plea. Veda was doing this to punish me, but I couldn't find it in myself to be upset with her, she was in the right. It felt like centuries before Veda let go of Dante's hands.

"Salvatore," he whispered.

I didn't dare speak, wanting him to digest what he learned about his past but also not wanting to bring attention to myself, fearing his wrath for messing with his memory.

"Thank you, Veda." Dante hugged her.

She was stuck in place, looking extremely small in his embrace. After a while she caved in, wrapping her arms around him to return the hug.

"I want to go home," Dante spoke to me in a monotone voice and with disgust in his eyes.

"Dante..." I grabbed his shoulder and he shrugged me off.

"Don't. Corvina, do that portal bullshit that you do and take me home. I don't want to be here anymore and certainly don't want to be around you for another second." He turned his back towards me.

I did as he asked, holding back tears as I did. Veda gave me a look of sympathy as Dante walked through the portal without saying another word or looking back to see if I was going back with him.

"He will forgive you. Just give him time, Corvina. This is a lot to come to terms with," Veda reassured me.

"It doesn't matter. My time in that world has ended. I'm coming home and taking what's mine, doing what I should've done months ago." I walked towards the portal.

"Corvina, you cannot do this without him," Veda warned.

"Just watch me."

Chapter Twenty-Eight

I t's been two days since I've heard from Dante. I swept the apartment one more time, making sure there wasn't anything that I was leaving behind. I was tempted to contact him to get my book back but decided against it. It was a stupid excuse and deep down I wanted him to keep it, to have something to remember me by.

Who am I kidding? He's not going to want to remember me.

As I checked under the bed a crumpled piece of paper caught my attention. I couldn't help but smile as I realized what it was, that stupid list of rules Dante had placed on the fridge door. I'm not sure how it made its way down here, I couldn't stop laughing as I read it.

Dante's DO's and DONT's

1. **<u>DON'T</u>** *touch Dante's wine collection*
2. **<u>DO</u>** *be tidy as Dante works hard to keep this place from falling apart.*
3. **<u>DON'T</u>** *touch any more of Dante's beer if you're going to just waste it.*
4. **<u>DO</u>** *keep in mind that Dante has a key so don't walk around the apartment naked. (No one wants to see that, gross).*
5. **<u>DON'T</u>** *under any circumstances fall in love with Dante. (It's*

*going to be hard because he's so charming and good looking
but you're a strong woman, you can resist.)*

Well, it looks like he thought too highly of my strength.

Holly has been trying to contact me non-stop. She didn't take my resignation text well. Her exact words were, *"Don't fuck with me Morticia. This isn't funny."* That text is the exact reason why I can't see her. She'll make me change my mind and my people need me.

There was a soft knock on my door that I was more than content to ignore until I heard her voice.

"Well, what are you waiting for? Open the damn door, or do you want me to go ape shit on your ass?" Her voice was stern.

Holly might be only five feet tall but something about that woman is terrifying. I opened the door and there she was, her face showing concern and anger. Behind her was Dante, refusing to make eye contact with me. Her big doe eyes were misty and I was not ready for the tears about to pour out of them.

"Please don't do this. I said my peace in the text. I need to go back home, for good." Holly's sadness quickly turned to rage.

"That's not good enough for me. You're not just my employee, you're my friend. You can't just up and leave, you didn't even give me a two-week notice. I don't accept your resignation." She stomped her high-heeled foot in protest.

"I'm leaving whether you accept it or not. I love you, Holly. Thank you for everything." I hugged her even though I knew she would protest and not hug me back.

"I know this is killing you. You know you want to, and I'm not letting go until you do." I kept a tight grip on her, knowing that she would eventually cave.

"Ugh fine." She hugged me so tight I could barely breathe.

"This has nothing to do with the grump behind me, does it? He's been extra moody these past couple of days. It's not good for business."

Dante made a move to leave.

"Oh no you don't, Dante. Move again and I swear." She didn't need to finish the threat for Dante to comply.

"We're fine. My leaving has nothing to do with either of you."

"I don't believe that for one second." She looked towards Dante's direction, making sure that he stood in place.

He was mindlessly scrolling through his phone as he leaned on the door frame. "I've been the same amount of crabby I've always been, sis."

The sound of his voice made my heart flutter.

"Both of you cut the crap and just tell me the damn truth. I had to drag your ass here. You two better fix whatever the fuck is going on or so help me God Dante Cole I'll fire you just to keep her around."

"You aren't my boss. I'm your partner, you can't fire me."

"Do you want to test that theory? Fix it!" Holly walked towards the door, pushing Dante inside the apartment and slamming the door behind her.

Dante might not want to look at me but I can't help but stare at him. His hair was hidden under his baseball cap, but I could tell he was wearing it to hide how disheveled it was underneath. Purple brimmed his eyes, telling me that he hadn't slept. His clothes were a wrinkled mess.

"I would leave but I know Holly is standing guard outside." He cleared his throat.

"You're damn right I am," Holly screamed through the door.

"Sorry for the inconvenience. I'll be out of your life soon

enough, just like you wanted."

Dante's neck snapped in my direction.

That comment got his attention.

"Holly, how can I talk to her if you're an earshot away? Leave."

"Fine, but I'm only going to the bottom of the stairs so if you start to yell I will hear you."We both heard her stomp away.

As soon as Dante was certain she wasn't within hearing distance he snapped.

"I forgot you're the expert in what I want. That's how you knew I wanted you to wipe away that memory right?" His jaw clenched as he spoke through his teeth.

"I was trying to protect you."

"Well, look who thinks I need their protection. The irony."

"You don't understand," I yelled at Dante.

"I hear yelling! Don't make me come up there," Holly screamed.

"We're fine!" We both yelled in unison.

I rubbed my temples, trying to calm down as Dante spoke.

"No, you don't understand. You took away a memory from me and messed with my brain with magic that until a couple of days ago I didn't even know existed. I didn't need your protection, I needed your honesty. When you aired out what you were, that would've been the perfect time but no, you decided to keep that little bit hidden from me. I trusted you."

"I'm sorry. I fucked up but everything I did was because I believed it was for the best. You think I wanted you to forget that? It was the last thing I wanted to do. My hands were tied, I had no choice. This conversation is redundant. It doesn't matter what's said because I'm still leaving."

"It matters to me. There's always a choice. Just because I

needed time to think shit through doesn't mean that I want you gone. I'm angry about the situation. I'm allowed to feel angry. You messed with my head and if I did the same to you wouldn't you be upset?" He enveloped me in his arms. I didn't realize that I was crying until I felt my body shake against his.

"I understand." I pulled myself from Dante's arms, grabbing a tissue from the side table.

"Please don't-" Dante was cut off by a portal opening up in the middle of the living room.

Veda made her way through the portal, closing it before she fell to the ground. Her robe was tattered and bloodied and as she looked up at me-I was horrified to see there was a hole in her skull where an eye used to be.

"Veda!" I ran to her, getting down on my knees to assess any further damage.

"Corvina, you must come now. They tried to capture me but I used the moves you taught me and escaped."

I had taught her a few basics of self-defense and I thank the Gods that I did.

"Oh, my Gods. What did they do to you, Veda?"

"Nothing I couldn't handle my sweet girl."

"Who did this to you?" Dante helped us both off the floor, guiding us to the couch.

"Royal guards. They attacked on your mother's orders. They want you, Corvina. They're going to do the coronation tonight. Someone tipped them off that you were on your way to take your place on the throne. Carmela will not let that happen. You must go, now!" Veda was still trying to catch her breath.

"Dante, keep an eye on her. I'll be back soon. I promise." My body became engulfed in purple flame, my fighting leathers still fit perfectly.

I grabbed the only physical weapon I had, my blade, and attached it to my thigh. The portal Veda entered through was now replaced by one that would get me to a cave where I hid weapons in case of emergencies. I felt a tug on my arm, Dante.

"No way in hell you're going without me."

"Dante now is not the time to be chivalrous. The little training I was able to give you will not be enough to stand by my side and fight. The last thing I need is for you to explode and injure not only me but yourself. Stay here." I urged him to let go of my arm but he refused.

"No. I'm going with you. I won't give you the chance to get yourself killed." His grip tightened with every word he said.

"Dante, you can think that all you want. You have no idea what you're up against. I will not intentionally put you in harm's way. Think about Holly. If anything happened to you I wouldn't be able to forgive myself." I hit a pressure point in his arm, forcing him to let me go. I made it halfway through the portal before Dante's words had me freezing in place.

"Yeah well, I love you too much to let you take on a suicide mission."

My throat closed up. Dante kept staring at me, with worried eyes as he waited for me to respond to his declaration. Veda cut the silence between us.

"Corvina, this is painful to watch and I only have one eye. This poor boy's heart is about to leap out of his chest. Are you going to confess your love or what?" Veda said with frustration.

"I'm just trying to make sure I heard him correctly. You love me?" My voice came out in a whisper.

"Yes. I love you Corvina. I love everything about you. Do you need me to list the ways? I will. I'll start with your wild hair, your snarky comments, and how you embraced my asshole tendencies. You're strong yet not afraid to show your emotions. You've brought a light to my life that's been missing. The list can go on for miles and if you let me keep going I will."

"You do love your lists," I mumbled.

"You finally read it."

"Yes, pendejo."

"I somehow find myself wanting to strangle you and kiss you at the same time." He grinded his teeth.

"You know, because of the types of books I read, both actions being done together sounds very appealing to me."

Dante laughed and my heart melted. "Oh trust me, I can have that arranged."

There's that fluttering in parts that aren't supposed to flutter.

"Corvina, you make me laugh in a way I haven't in years. I wanted to deny my feelings for you, ashamed that I could see anyone romantically after Adeline, but the more I spent time with you the more I thought that maybe she brought you to me."

My cheeks started to hurt from all of my smiling. In front of me was a man who loved me for me. He loved everything I was as just me, not because I was royalty. He didn't see me as a business opportunity, a way to increase his power or social status. My chest felt full like at any moment I might burst. I am enough in his eyes and for that, I am forever grateful.

Dante Pendejo Cole loves me back.

My body moved on its own accord, running into Dante and kissing him. As soon as our bodies collided it felt like two puzzle pieces that fit perfectly together. I could kiss him for centuries and I would've if Veda didn't clear her throat.

"Te amo," I confessed as Dante caressed my cheek.

"You broke rule number five." He smirked.

"I can always take it back." I tried to pull away, making Dante's hold on me stronger.

"Yo también te amo," he replied.

"Have you been practicing that in the mirror to yourself or?"

"Of course, I always tell myself how much I love myself in the mirror and only in Spanish."

We both laughed before locking lips again.

"Sorry to interrupt. I'm very happy for you both, but must I remind you that I'm here before any piece of clothing starts to be discarded? Also, no rush, but the Shadow Court is waiting for you to save them."

Our lips separated and we both smiled as though my world wasn't falling apart as we stood there like lovestruck idiots.

"Please. You don't have to do this alone." Dante pleaded.

"This isn't your duty, it's mine. I ran away from my responsibilities and though it led me to you, it was wrong. I need to go fix it." I kissed the palm of his hand.

"Promise me you'll come back. I can't lose you."

"Cross my heart and hope I don't die." I smiled at him, knowing that I meant what I said. I will make it back to him.

"Hey! That's my line, get your own Princesa Corvina." He smoothed the top of my hair before kissing my forehead.

I walked backward towards the portal, wanting Dante to be the last thing I saw.

"That's Reina Corvina to you, Mr. Cole."

I blew him a kiss and as I did, I hoped I could make good on my promise and come back to him.

Chapter Twenty-Nine

eep breath. Take a deep breath and walk through the door like you own the place because technically you do. Don't be a little pendeja.

"You are Corvina Morticia Umbra, queen of the Shadow Court and they will bow down to you," I whispered to myself

That pep talk did nothing for my nerves. My body stood in place, the palace seemed bigger than I remembered. My sword hung snugly against my back, feeling heavier by the minute. Who was I fooling, trying to take my place as queen, fighting against her? She trained me and knows all of my weaknesses. Maybe she will be willing to bow out gracefully, though she has never backed down from a fight before in her centuries of existence. Does she have it in her to fight her daughter?

Who am I kidding of course she does. The real question is, would she?

"Hey!" A guard screamed from across the courtyard.

Mierda.

I rushed through the double doors. There was no turning back now, he would soon alert the rest of the guards about the intruder. The hunt for me has begun. I ran towards my parents' room, hoping she was in there. These hallways seemed to go for miles, I was starting to think that I would never make it to their bedroom door. I'm trying to take deep breaths but it's not working. My lungs are desperate for air that isn't coming. It's as though there are hands wrapped around my throat, slowly choking the life out of me. I leaned forward on the door frame, the lack of oxygen starting to blur my vision. A gust of wind hits my face as the door opens and a full head of chestnut brown curls greets me.

Her hand slowly caresses my cheek as she whispers, "Princesa, perdóname."

Mami's voice was the last thing I heard before the darkness claimed me.

Chapter Thirty

Concrete walls greeted me as I woke up, steel bars caged me in. My hands burned as they wrapped around the iron bars, an enchantment placed on them to keep me in. I wanted to scream but I knew it would be a useless tactic, it would land on deaf ears. I recognized where I was the moment I opened my eyes. I had only been here once before, but what I witnessed would scar me for life. Only the worst of the worst were captured and thrown down here, the only place fit enough to house them. Papi's magic is what holds this place together, he made it so that even after his death it will still hold. If legend holds, there is no escaping here.

I threw all my power at the bars but nothing seemed to work. My breathing started to shallow at the thought of this being my new home, my new life as a prisoner because no one could rescue me.

They shouldn't have to. You should be better than this, you were trained better than this. Figure out how to get out of here Corvina.

My eyes scanned my surroundings again, looking for anything to help me escape. Maybe there was a crack in the concert foundation that I could hit in a way to make a hole?

There's nothing.

How pathetic that I was so easily captured. Add this to the

list of things Papi would be disappointed in me for. He's rolling around in his grave right now, the thought of his disappointment is making me sick. Maybe Veda was right, I'm a fool for thinking I could do this on my own. His own daughter, his own blood was unable to escape the prison he created.

His blood... That's it!

I unsheathed my blade, those fools didn't even think to disarm me, they thought so little of me and my ability to find a way out. The palms of my hands stung as I broke my skin. I gripped the bars with my bloody hands.

If my father's blood created this place, it could also destroy the spell holding me here right?

My skin melted against the iron as I held on, using what little strength and hope I had left. Nothing was happening, my theory didn't work. Either it was a long shot or I'm just not strong enough. I was about to let go and officially give up hope when the bars started to shake, as though they were unsure if they should let their captive out or not. I squeezed the bars harder, the smell of my burning flesh becoming nauseating.

Blood trickled down my arm as I spoke, "I am the heir of Castro Umbra. His blood is my blood. Release me now, release the rightful queen of Aebriera."

My body hit the ground with a big thud as the iron bars disappeared and my exhaustion consumed me. I laid on my back, enjoying the cold concrete floor against my boiling-hot skin, and just laughed, shocked that my plan actually worked.

The shock quickly wore off when I heard a familiar voice in the distance. My jaw clenched as I tried to control my rage. I clung my body against the wall as I walked towards his voice, making sure I had eyes on him without him having a view of me. As I caught sight of him it was hard not to attack, as much as I would love nothing more than to feel the stickiness of his blood splattered on my skin.

Well, that's a new feeling. I've never felt murderous rage before. Not sure if I like that.

"Just remember you're not to cause any harm to Corvina unless you want a slow and painful death. You can have fun with these two, especially him." Elias pointed at someone that was out of my view.

"You can torture him as much as you want." He scowled, spitting at the prisoner as he walked away.

How generous of him to spare me of torture. I, however, won't be so kind once I get my hands on him.

I gave myself a mental pat on the back for coming to my senses and breaking our engagement. When I get my hands on him I will make it my mission to give him the beating he rightfully deserves.

Death would be too merciful. Oh, my Gods. I'm turning into Papi.

"What about your father sir?" the guard asked.

"Just make sure he is comfortable, I will be back later to check on him."

Clemente Murano is here as a prisoner. Elias must be loving this.

"Yes sir, it will be an honor to be at your service."

"Get your lips off my ass, would you. I've only been head of the Royal Guard for an hour."

Yup, he's definitely loving this. Look who got what he always wanted.

My hands balled into fists beside me as I refocused on the task at hand: trying to find my way out. I could follow Elias in hopes he was heading back to the palace but the risk of him catching on that he's being followed is too high. There are no distinct features on the walls to distinguish if I've been down this specific one already, for all I knew I was walking around in circles. I tried my best to ignore the cells and who they were housing. Plenty of them tried to grab my attention, most growled at my presence or spoke in a tongue I couldn't understand. My frustration was building.

Smart enough to get out of my cell but can't find the door to get out of this fucking place. Estupida.

"Psst." I ignored that whisper like I'd done with the rest of the lost souls begging for my attention.

Whoever that was, whatever it was, they were not to be trusted.

"Psst, over here, Princess. I know you can hear my whispers," the voice kept baiting me.

Ignore it, Corvina. Just keep going.

Another turn into a dead end.

"Are you fucking kidding me?" I snarled.

"Princess, I can get you out. Follow the sound of my voice. Puedo ayudarte, lo prometo."

I can feel time slipping away and so is my common sense.

Of course, they're going to promise to help you, Corvina. Are you that desperate to actually believe them? Yes, yes I am. Gods, please don't let this be a mistake.

Going against my better judgment, I followed the whispers. My skin became clammy and my body stiffened as soon as I stared it in the eyes. I tried to calm my breathing, as it became shallow and rapid.

This is a mistake. A horrible, terrible mistake.

The resemblance was terrifying, the spitting image of myself looked deep into my soul. I've read about this creature in books but never had the misfortune to meet one in person. The stories about the Delphis are horrendous. A nasty creature of trickery, bribery, and deceit. They show you the worst parts of yourself to scare you into doing their bidding. With one look at you, they know your worst fears, whispering promises in your ear, ones that they can fulfill but it's always at a cost.

Remember Corvina, there is always a price to pay.

A Delphis never reveals its true form, they only take the form of their victim. It's well known that making a deal with one is dangerous, but some faes do it anyway when they're desperate.

I will not become one of them.

"Are you scared of what you see, Princess? You shouldn't be. You're going to make a glorious queen." The Delphis twirled in its cell so I could get a full view.

If you didn't personally know me then you would be easily fooled by what the Delphis showed you. Its only flaw was that there was darkness to what I was seeing, there was no light in its eyes. Papi had a crown made for me to wear when the time came, that crown now laid on top of the Delphis' head. Its curly hair was up in an elegant bun, with curls framing its face. A black dress clung to every curve on its body and a crushed velvet red corset cinched at its waist. The smile on its face was wicked.

"I'm not scared, just shocked. Legend has it that your skills of shape-shifting are immaculate. Yet as I look at you, your depiction of me is inaccurate." I gasped as it flung itself to the front of the prison cell.

An arm squeezed between the bars, hand sprawled out desperate to reach me. It grabbed onto the bars, its skin burned just as mine did yet there was no sign of pain on its face.

"Don't ever doubt my abilities, Princess. My reflection of you is just fine, you aren't quite there yet on your journey. I am the perfect mirror image." The Delphis snarled at me, showing me its teeth.

"I'm not sure what journey you saw but it wasn't mine. I will never be or look as wicked as you do right now."

"You say this, yet weren't you just thinking about murder a couple of seconds ago?"

How did it know that?

It cackled before speaking again. "If you believe that is your truth. It would be rude of me to break that delusion."

"You said if I followed your voice you would help me. Here I am. Now what is your price?"

"Lovely to hear that you are well educated on my species."

"Spit it out before I change my mind." I threated.

"My freedom is the price you'll pay. If you don't pay them you will never get out and you will become what you fear the most." The smell of the Delphis skin burning was suffocating me.

"You do not get to tell me about my fears or what I will become. I am more than capable of creating my destiny. I am not one of those desperate faes on which you can do your trickery. Do not underestimate me."

"If you say so. I have Oracle friends of my own, you know. Your friend is not being one hundred percent honest with you. Do not blame me if you end up like your mother."

I will not let it rile me up, that is what it wants.

"Do not speak of her as though you know her, you foul creature."

"You shouldn't speak to yourself that way, it's unbecoming. Princess, I might not know her but neither do you. You didn't think she would ever put you in harm's way yet here you are." The Delphis began to twirl a loose curl around its finger as it baited me.

"I refuse to believe a word that comes from your horrid mouth."

"That is not a wise choice. I am not as horrible as you think me to be. As a kind gesture, I will help lead the way to your freedom so you can hear the truth from the source."

The Delphis walked through the walls of its cell with ease, making me gasp. It smiled as it walked me through the halls.

"Not everything is always as it seems, Princess. I am no prisoner. Your father made it so I can leave whenever I like. He liked the idea of his men having to catch the freed prisoners as a drill and I find it more fun to make deals with those who are longing for freedom."

This will end once I am queen, but no need to let the Delphis know that before they can help me.

"You are a cruel thing."

"Thank you." The Delphis halted once we reached the door that would set me free.

I pushed my way through the door before it decided to have a change of heart.

"You're no use to me as a Princess so come back to me when you are queen. Then we can have a nice chat."

A slight breeze tickled the back of my neck, the Delphis had disappeared before I could thank it. I was left wondering what exactly it was they wanted to have a chat about.

Chapter Thirty-One

Earlier this year I decided to run away; a decision that was not only selfish but also reckless. Even though I made that decision with no malice in my heart, it has caused great pain for myself and my people. I've never thought I was good enough. Always under the impression that I would be a horrible queen, but my self-doubt isn't my reality. How would I know if I didn't try? So that's what I'm going to do.

No more running, no more self-doubt. It's time for me to become queen and implement the necessary changes to improve this court.

I regret all the pain it's caused, regret not being able to say my goodbye to the man who raised me but what a journey it was. My journey brought me to Dante and Holly, in that regard my cowardliness did me well.

The rumbling inside echoed in my ear, my body tensed knowing that my people were behind that door. Will they be happy to see me or turn against me for turning my back on them? There's a possibility that the Shadow Court will reject me out of spite for what I have done. I adjusted my posture as I prepared for what was waiting behind those doors, holding my head high, my life to be forever changed.

"Here goes nothing," I mumbled as the doors swung open.

All eyes were on me and as I walked down the aisle towards

the throne I could hear the whispers but none of them pulled my focus away from her. Neither of us spoke a word, our eyes locked onto one another. The only communication she gave was a flick of her wrist, directed towards her guards to lower their weapons.

"Look who has decided to grace us all with her presence. It's the runaway fae herself. " There was venom spewing from Mami's voice.

The woman I stared at looked like Mami but there was an energy pulsing from her that felt wrong.

"What a warm welcome. I'm doing well, by the way, thanks for asking. The correct moment to ask me how I was doing was before throwing me into a prison cell."

"I suggest you grab a seat before I have one of my men place you back in that cell."

"You're delusional if you think I am going to take a seat and watch you take my crown." I moved closer, making her guards raise their weapons once again.

"Oh, so now it's *your crown*. Your purpose in leaving was to make me queen, was it not? So because you're regretting that decision I'm supposed to bow out? I don't think so, Corvina. You made your bed, now you must lie in it." She got up from the throne and walked down the stairs toward me.

My knees wanted to buckle but I fought the urge to cave in, refusing to let her presence affect me even though the closer she got to me, the more it felt like the oxygen in the room was thinning.

"I should have never left the crown to you, I see that now. These people deserve to be led by the rightful heir to the throne and not someone who stabbed their king in the chest!" My voice was rough as I screamed.

Gasps filled the room and once again whispers echoed throughout.

"My Whispering Delirium plan had gone so well, the healer was easily persuaded to give him a false diagnosis."

The whole room was silenced, the only sound I could hear was the beating of my heart.

"The confusion on your face is priceless." She pinched my chin between her fingers.

"I'm happy to enlighten you. You see Corvina, it's I who is destined for this crown, not you. I've done everything in my power to ensure that I get what I rightfully deserve. You're not the only one with oracle friends, mine told me that I would be the queen of the Shadow Court and since that day I've worked hard to make sure this court is mine and mine alone to rule." She circled me as a hunter does with their prey.

"With the help of a witch friend of mine, I cast a spell to make Castro fall in love with me. He never stood a chance. Since the day we married, I've been calling all of the shots, making every decision for this court. It was so easy under the spell's influence to plant ideas in his little head about how to rule. The one flaw I had in my plan was you." She stopped behind me, using her index finger to brush my hair from my neck.

"I never wanted children, let alone a daughter. No matter how hard I tried to get Castro to forget the idea of having a child he would not budge. Unfortunately marrying royalty means providing them with an heir, so I reluctantly gave birth to you and you became Castro's world. Corvina this and Corvina that. He couldn't get enough of you. It was nauseating. I once again received help from my witch friend to ensure after your birth that I would no longer be capable of having children. Though your presence was annoying, I was grateful for it. You were the perfect distraction for Castro. Your birth allowed me the opportunity to have fewer eyes on me as I worked on obtaining the crown."

My eyes began to sting. I tried to hold back my tears but the more she talked, the more she revealed her true self to me, the more my body took over and they spilled onto my face. A mixture of anger and sadness consumed me. The realization of how truly evil she is sank in. I never thought I would want to end the life of anyone, let alone the woman who gave me life, yet here I was planning all the ways I could kill her without feeling an ounce of remorse.

"I had to think quickly. Now there was an heir and the crown would rightfully belong to you. How could I become queen with you still around? It was a struggle but then it hit me, you were the answer. A person can be their own worst enemy, I must plant a seed of self-doubt in your mind. Convince you that you were not fit to be queen and make you not want your crown. If I could get you to fear the crown then it would leave no one else but me around to claim it. I would say it worked like a charm. I'd never been happier to see your runaway letter, everything has fallen into place perfectly."

She did this. She made me feel unworthy.

"How can you be so wicked and cruel? Is power really that important to you?"

"Oh darling, you want to rule yet you're still so naive. Power is everything. I grew up with nothing. I didn't want to become a warrior and see all the horrors that I did but it had to be done to get what I wanted. Power, money, loyal subjects- that is what I craved and now I have it all." She threw up her hands as an evil grin took over her face.

"Without that power, Corvina, I couldn't do this."

Carmela's hand flew to my throat, cutting off my airway. Her power infected my veins like a poison. She paralyzed me, my body was limp and unable to move.

"Now that we have that settled, we can continue with my coronation." She lifted me by my throat and tossed me across the room.

My head hit the brick wall and I could feel the blood trickling down the back of my skull.

"Unless anyone in this room objects to me becoming their queen?"

Complete silence.

"Lovely. Now, since I am a kind and just queen I'll know a little secret: your life is now linked to mine. What's done to me is done to you. I die, you die. Just wanted to let you know in case you wanted to try to harm your poor Mami in any way."

Did she think I was scared of death? I laughed. She might've given birth to me and might have planted ideas in my head, but she didn't know me at all. If it meant that she would be gone from this world then I would gladly sacrifice myself and haunt her in the afterlife. The fury on Carmela's face grew as my laugh continued.

"I'm glad you find this amusing because the real fun is about to begin."

My laughing came to a halt as soon as the doors opened. His face was bloodied and bruised, his bottom lip swollen and dawning a huge gash. Where fear should've been there was pure rage and as Dante's green eyes met mine his face softened. A flash of red hair caught my attention, her body flailing around to fight off the guard that held her.

"You son of a bitch. LET ME GO!" Holly screamed at the top of her lungs, her pale skin turning as red as her hair.

She found her opening and attacked, biting the guard.

"You bitch!" the guard yelled.

"Don't talk to her like that, I swear to God I'm going to kill you," Dante growled.

"I've got this Dante... I swear to God I'm going to kill you," Holly snarled.

Dante and Holly were thrown to the floor, kneeling before Carmela. She caressed the top of Holly's head and brushed her hand through Dante's beard. I snarled as she touched him.

"Ah, you do have a soft spot for this one. Elias told me you had a human plaything but it was hard to believe that you could have eyes for anyone but him. I mean Elias is the definition of the perfect specimen. It was such a stroke of luck that he was part of Castro's guards and had feelings for you. I was ecstatic to test the theory: Would love win over the promise of power?" Elias appeared beside her, grinning at the view of Dante helplessly on his knees.

"Well, we both know how that turned out. Like I said Corvina, power is everything, it even triumphs love."

"You're just bitter because no one has ever loved you." Holly spit at Carmela's feet.

"Tell that to Elias. He said he loved me a lot while he warmed my bed."

"How could you?" I whispered to Elias.

"I must serve my kingdom. It is my duty just like it was yours. You might have forgotten that but I never did. I offered you a chance to fix it, to come back home with me. You made your choice, so I made mine," he replied.

Carmela took the sword from Elias' waist, kissing his cheek before placing its tip at Holly's throat. "Love makes you stupid. Love gets you into situations like this, where you die."

"Touch her and you'll be signing up for your death," Dante growled.

Carmela grinned, "Oh, this is going to be fun."

She dragged Holly by her hair, tossing her at the base of the stairs. She hovered behind her with the sword at her throat. Carmela's attention turned to me, making my stomach churn. Her hand reached towards me, directing her magic to force me to my feet and dragging me next to Holly.

"Choose," she told Dante.

He refused to speak. Carmela applied more pressure onto the sword causing Holly to whimper as she bled.

"The only way I will choose is if you're an option!" he screamed.

Carmela moved the sword from Holly's throat to mine. "So then you have chosen. If I kill Corvina it will also kill me. So you'll get what you want but at the expense of losing her."

"Just let them go. Unlink me and you can do with me what you want. You have my word." I closed my eyes, waiting for the Gods to take me.

"That's no fun. I want him to choose. Your sister or Corvina. Would you prefer it if I chose for you?"

Dante hung his head, refusing to look up at Holly and me. His tears were hitting the tile floor as his body shook from his sobs.

"Por favor, no hagas esto." I pleaded.

"It's un queen-like to beg Corvina. This is happening. The clock is ticking Dante. Choose."

"I chose me. Kill me." Dante extended his neck, offering it to Carmela.

"Tu no escuchas. I hate when people don't listen."

Dante started to fight back, but more guards began to restrain him.

Carmela yawned. "Times up. I get to choose and I choose you."

"Nooo!" I screamed as she slit Holly's throat and a waterfall of blood covered her neck.

Dante wailed. I couldn't bring myself to look at him knowing that this was all my fault. Holly would still be alive, living life and growing old with the woman she loves. Dante would still have his sister. Carmela swiped her finger across the sword, covering it in Holly's blood. Her now bloodied index finger disappeared in her mouth, making a popping nose as she removed it, sucking it clean. Dante was shaking, if there was ever an appropriate time for Dante to explode it would be right now.

"I feel rotten, I do. Not about killing Holly, honestly that's the most excitement I've had in years."

Carmela bent down to whisper, "I feel rotten about lying to you. We aren't linked."

"Cabróna." I spat at her.

"Don't bother praying to the Gods. If they gave a shit about you, they wouldn't have made me your mother."

Dante's cry was the last thing I heard before the darkness swallowed me.

Chapter Thirty-Two

The definition of darkness is the absence of light. What I'm currently experiencing is something darker than darkness itself. Gasping for air, my hands gripped my burning throat and I could feel the dried-up blood crumble beneath my touch. That bitch killed me! Mami slit my throat without hesitation and forced Dante to watch. I could care less about my own life, but to have Dante witness yet another death of someone he loves is making my heart ache. Two more people in his life are dead and because of me more pain and misery have entered his life. That is if Carmela hasn't ended it already.

The sight of Holly before she took her last breath replayed in my head. It was the only thing I could see in this abyss and I'm sure this is the Gods punishment for me. I jumped to my feet calling out to Dante and Holly, wondering if they had joined me in the afterlife.

Do humans and fae coexist in the afterlife?

I was unsure but wouldn't give up trying to find them, or anyone.

"Please, can anyone hear me?" As I asked, a flicker of light appeared before me, the bright orb dodging all my advances to try and capture it.

My eyes went into a frenzy as it circled its way around me.

More of them appeared, following the first one's lead. They wrapped around me and as they did my body floated up in the air, my tattered clothing replaced with a beautiful white floor-length gown. My body was radiating light, and all of the scars that followed me into death were cleared from my skin.

I thanked them, even though I was unsure if the light could understand me.

A beam of light appeared across from me. It was as if someone had opened a pathway out of this dreaded place. My new friends helped lead the way. My desperation to not be alone made me trust them, so I followed. I knew I shouldn't, but part of me knew they wouldn't lead me into harm's way. This path felt like peace and serenity. Though I don't deserve those feelings, I wanted them. I might not have been the one who wielded the sword that ended Holly's life but I inserted myself into her and Dante's lives and no matter how much joy they brought me, that joy wasn't worth all of the suffering.

The sweat on my palms started to collect, my stomach fluttering. I stepped into the light and just like that there was no darkness. My newfound friends disappeared and I was once again all alone. I had read my fair share of books about the afterlife. No one book was the same, however they all had one thing in common. They all spoke of the Gods: Tassia, the Goddess of War; Damaris, the Goddess of life and Nature; Arad, the God of Knowledge; Astra, the Goddess of the Moon and Stars; Kessem, the God of Afterlife. They spoke of how they would judge our lives and decide how we deserve to spend the rest of our eternity. I looked around, desperate to find a way out of here, unsure that if I did find one it would be better than here. I checked the white walls surrounding me, hoping that I could find a secret passageway. I've never truly felt completely hopeless until this very moment, where not even magic could save me, but maybe the Gods could still hear my pleas.

"I know that I have disgraced you all. I've blamed you all for my shortcomings. I'm sorry. I realize that I was born into a privileged life, I mean I'm a fucking princess. Oops, sorry, language." I took a deep breath and started again.

"I am the Princess of the Shadow Court, or I was... and I should've seen that as a privilege instead of a curse. Instead of honing in on my powers and responsibilities, I failed to lead and now my court is in disarray. I should've seen Carmela's deception. Please give me another chance at that life. I will live it the way it was meant to be lived. Make the Shadow Court a better place, have the people there and my Papi proud of me. All I've wanted was to be the daughter he deserved. I want to be worthy of the love he gave me."

I shuddered as a cool breeze blew through my hair and a hand grazed my shoulder.

"You have always been worthy of my love." His silky voice was music to my ears.

"Papi?" I sobbed into his chest as he pulled me into his embrace.

"No llores mi amor." He wiped away the tears.

What an impossible task, to not cry. He looked exactly as he did the day I left, the way he's looked my entire life. His long black hair was full of shine, his beard peppered with sprinkles of gray hairs.

"Please don't leave me again. I'm so sorry, Papi."

"I would never leave you. I might not be there physically but I'm always in your heart."

His slender hand reached for mine. I held onto it tightly, afraid to let it go.

CHAPTER THIRTY-TWO

"Mami, she tricked you. She put a spell to –"

Papi put his hand up to stop me. "I know. Once I had passed to this side, everything was revealed to me. I let our people down by letting her inside our walls but you have the power to stop it all."

"I was able to see my whole life from a different perspective. I understand why you didn't want to rule. The cruelty that I displayed as a king was uncalled for. Though it was not fully my doing, but Carmela's, I wonder what the Shadow Court would be if it was led with love instead of fear. If I was strong enough to not fall for her trickery."

"You are the strongest person I know Papi. It's not your fault."

"Just like it is not your fault that Carmela is evil and placed doubt in your head."

"I love you, Papi."

"I've had many titles during my lifetime. King, warrior, and husband, but my greatest title has been being your father. Corvina, you are the best thing that has ever happened to me. You can change the path of the Shadow Court, but to do that we have to get you home." He kissed my forehead.

"She took a sword to my throat, how is there any coming back from that?"

"I saw that and I wish that I could be the one to slice her throat for it but I know you will make her pay. When you do make sure it's in my honor. Kessem has gifted me a chance to take you home."

Why did Kessem give him this gift?

"Can he grant me my wish of taking you with me?"

"My love will be with you, always, but I must stay here. Now give Carmela the ass-kicking she deserves."

The woman I once called my mother loves to say that power is everything. How it's better than love, but she's wrong. Carmela is about to find that out the hard way. She took the people I love from me and I will not stop until I get my revenge.

My name is Corvina Morticia Umbra, daughter of Castro Umbra, and I am the queen of Aebriera.

The End... For now.

Acknowledgments

It's hard to believe that I am writing an acknowledgments page for my novel. Every person I am about to talk about has been a crucial part of the making of this book and has helped make this dream a reality.

Louis Angel Lemus, my amazing husband, you are my rock. You're the man who has been so understanding and supportive on this journey. Thank you for constantly calming my fears and anxieties about releasing my story for the world to see. You always remind me that I am more than good enough. I promise you'll have a book of mine dedicated to you. I won't let you know which one, you know I love to keep you on your toes.

Thank you to my mother for raising me into the reader and writer I am today. I will always remember the summer you had to take the new *Twilight* book away from me so that I could play outside. I promise that one day I will be able to pay you back for all the school book fair money you gave me as a kid.

Annalise, thank you for enjoying the world of fantasy and romance books as much as I do. I appreciate you always being down to film content and exploring new bookstores with me.

When I told my friends I was writing a book I was terrified. As I told them, I was met with nothing but encouraging words. Thank you to everyone who read excerpts of the book and gave me constructive and honest feedback: Victoria, Sophia, Hailey, Sydney, Maria, and Alex. A million thanks to those who allowed me to film them for publicity: Jamila, Jessica, Talya, and Stormy.

Allison, my self-appointed editor and friend, thank you for helping me edit this book and being the person I could turn to for ideas. Your genuine reactions made me even more excited to continue writing this book and for the world to see it. While editing this book I asked a lot of you, but I'm going to ask for one more thing: Please be available to edit the next book and all future books.

Finally, thank you to everyone who picked up this book. You have made a woman who never thought her writing dream could come true so happy. I appreciate you all for diving into this world that I created.

This is starting to feel like an award speech and the music is playing me off the stage. I'm so sorry if I forgot anyone, I love you all, and thank you for reading book one of the Aebriera trilogy. See you soon!

About the Author

Tamara Lemus discovered her passion for writing at a young age, sparked by the gift of journals from her mother. Later, she branched out onto the online writing scene by writing *Harry Styles* fan fiction on *Tumblr*. Her love of reading started when a little book titled *Twilight* entered the world. As life became more demanding, reading fell to the back burner, but the moment she picked up a book again, she was hooked once again. Today, Tamara enjoys diving into fantasy, romance, and thrillers. In her free time, she loves to travel, explore new cuisines, and spend quality time with her family and her beloved fur baby, Xena.